STRONG-BLOODED YOUNG MEN AND WOMEN EVERYWHERE HAVE ALSO READ THESE OTHER THRILLING TALES OF PALS IN PERIL

Whales on Stilts!

The Clue of the Linoleum Lederhosen

Jasper Dash and the Flame-Pits of Delaware

Agent Q, or The Smell of Danger!

A Pals in Peril Tale

ZOMBIE MOMMY

M. T. ANDERSON

Illustrations by KURT CYRUS

BEACH LANE BOOKS

NEW YORK   LONDON

TORONTO   SYDNEY   NEW DELHI

To my mother

BEACH LANE BOOKS
An imprint of Simon & Schuster Children's Publishing Division
1230 Avenue of the Americas, New York, New York 10020
This book is a work of fiction. Any references to historical events, real people,
or real locales are used fictitiously. Other names, characters, places, and incidents
are products of the author's imagination, and any resemblance to actual events
or locales or persons, living or dead, is entirely coincidental.
Text copyright © 2011 by M. T. Anderson
Illustrations copyright © 2011 by Kurt Cyrus
All rights reserved, including the right of reproduction
in whole or in part in any form.
BEACH LANE BOOKS is a trademark of Simon & Schuster, Inc.
For information about special discounts for bulk purchases, please contact
Simon & Schuster Special Sales at 1-866-506-1949
or business@simonandschuster.com.
The Simon & Schuster Speakers Bureau can bring authors to your live event.
For more information or to book an event, contact the Simon & Schuster Speakers Bureau
at 1-866-248-3049 or visit our website at www.simonspeakers.com.
Also available in a Beach Lane Books hardcover edition
The text for this book is set in Stempel Garamond.
Manufactured in the United States of America
0812 OFF
First Beach Lane Books paperback edition September 2012
2 4 6 8 10 9 7 5 3 1
Library of Congress Cataloging-in-Publication Data
Anderson, M. T.
Zombie mommy / M. T. Anderson ; illustrations by Kurt Cyrus. — 1st ed.
p. cm. — (A pals in peril tale)
Summary: Home from their latest Delaware crime-stopping adventures,
Lily Gefelty and her friends Katie, Jasper, and Drgnan Pghlik face killer tarantulas
and teenaged vampires when they try to rescue Lily's mother, who has been possessed
by a menacing zombie that wants to take over the world.
ISBN 978-1-4169-8641-6 (hardcover)
ISBN 978-1-4391-5610-0 (eBook)
[1. Adventure and adventurers—Fiction. 2. Zombies—Fiction. 3. Humorous stories.]
I. Cyrus, Kurt, ill. II. Title.
PZ7.A54395Zo 2011
[Fic]—dc22
2010047668
ISBN 978-1-4424-5440-8 (pbk)

1

Sometimes things are dead, but still move.

I mean the leaves, of course. The leaves of autumn.

They crawled across the basketball court, scuttling sideways with the wind, tripping and pouncing. It was late fall. Almost everything was dead or hiding. The frogs were dead, the fish were dead, the bugs were dead, and the birds had escaped to Boca Raton.

The sky was not dead, however. It was blue and active. Clouds rolled across it. Trees in vacant lots scratched at it. And in the middle of all the creeping leaves and the nude, shivering branches of dead trees, Lily Gefelty and her mother sat in a car, waiting for Lily's friends to arrive so the kids could play basketball.

Lily and her mother were having a difficult conversation.

"We need to talk," said Mrs. Gefelty.

"Okay," said Lily. "But everyone else is going to be here in a minute."

"That's fine. But we need to have a, you know, heart-to-heart."

"About what?"

"About books."

A book discussion doesn't sound like it should be a difficult conversation, but it was for the Gefeltys. This was because Lily had actually *been in* several books recently. For instance, this one.

Lily had gone through most of her life without appearing in any books at all. Most of us never do. Though some of her friends had appeared in books, Lily had always liked the fact that she had stayed behind the scenes, because she was a pretty shy person and she didn't think her life was very interesting. Then she began to show up in this series, Pals in Peril. People from the publishing company would call and get details of her adventures, then they would write them up and publish them. It was a little strange for her at first, but she got used to it.

Her mother was still getting used to it.

Mrs. Gefelty sat there in the driver's seat, looking anxious. She tapped on the steering wheel and looked into the rearview mirror at the backseat. It was filled with library books. Mrs. Gefelty stared at them as if they were poisonous snakes that might strike at any time.

"Lily," she said, "have you read the books you're assigned for school?"

Lily looked at her mother, shocked. She always did all her homework. "Mom!" she said. "Of course!"

"Have you noticed anything about books written for people your age?" Her mother clearly was waiting for a particular answer.

Lily shrugged. "It's a bad idea to have a horse?" she guessed.

"It is a bad idea," said her mother, "*to have a mother*." She pressed her forehead with the heel of her hand and sighed. "In every single book your English teacher assigns you, the mother dies or disappears." She reached back and began shuffling through the stack of books that slid on the backseat cushions. "In this one, the mother contracts cholera. In this one, she dies of cancer. In this one, she's killed in a rogue trolley accident. In this one, she's eaten by a rhinoceros. In this one, she's making stew when the pressure cooker blows up. And in *this* one," Lily's mother exclaimed, throwing a particularly heavy, dismal-looking volume down on Lily's lap, "she goes to a *dance party* and catches *the smallpox. WHAT ARE THESE PEOPLE THINKING?*"

Lily didn't know what to say. She shrugged.

Mrs. Gefelty demanded, "What do they have against mothers?"

Lily couldn't answer that one either. Now that she thought about it, the mothers in books didn't have such great luck with disease, electricity, the ocean, or crosswalks.

Then Lily realized what was really bugging her mom . . . and a second later, Mrs. Gefelty herself said it: "So what am I supposed to think? Now that you are showing up in books? See what I mean? Do I have to start worrying?"

"Mom, the books I'm in are different," said Lily. "The ones you're reading aren't true. My stories really, actually happened to me."

"Who knows? Maybe I'm next." Mrs. Gefelty pressed her hands together between her knees. She was frowning. "I've made an appointment to have a checkup with Dr. Singh tomorrow." She scratched the back of her head, as if she felt a sudden, unaccountable itch. "And we've got to get a burglar alarm in the house. And a radon gas sensor. And motion detectors." Mrs. Gefelty snapped her fingers. "Hey, do you think the fire alarms need new batteries?" She pointed at Lily. "Chore!" she said. "Check them all. Buy batteries. Replace any old ones." She dusted off the dashboard anxiously. "I'm going to go home and go through the medicine cabinet and throw away everything that's past its sell-by date. You never know when vitamin D will turn weird."

"Mom, I think you might be overreacting."

Mrs. Gefelty insisted, "Disaster is hanging over my head. We have got to do everything we can to avoid it."

Lily's friends were pulling up and getting out of the back doors of cars.

Lily said, "I wouldn't worry about it, Mom."

"I'll try not to," said Mrs. Gefelty, worrying. She stared into the distance.

Lily leaned over and gave her a kiss. Mrs. Gefelty jumped as if startled. "Oh," she said, and smiled awkwardly.

As Lily walked over to greet her friends, her mother drove off to arrange protection against any unforeseen and dire circumstances. As Mrs. Gefelty's car rounded the corner, she gave a sweet smile and waved back to her daughter.

But you've read this book's title.

You know tough times are coming for Mrs. G.

So get ready. If we stick together, we might all just make it through this thing alive.

2

Lily was worried about her mom.

But for the moment, she was more worried about the basketball game.

She was trying to stop her friend Katie Mulligan from getting the ball.

"Jas!" screamed Katie. "Pass!"

Jasper Dash, Boy Technonaut, wheeled his elbows around, trying to shoot over his friend Drgnan Pghlik's waving hands so he could get the ball to Katie.

Jasper chucked the ball. It bounced once. Katie grabbed it and dribbled for the basket.

Lily, puffing, ran after her. It was Lily's job to keep Katie covered, and she never could do it. Katie was much faster than her.

Lily did not like playing basketball. It embarrassed her deeply. Her friends were pretty athletic—Drgnan Pghlik, for example, was a magical monk, a holy boy capable of hovering forty or fifty feet over mountainsides (under the right circumstances), and Jasper Dash had dodged laser bolts shot by secret robots in all the countries of Eastern Europe. Katie was pretty much in shape too. She didn't know martial arts like the boys, but she played soccer, ran track, and wrestled with newts from Beyond.

Since we're talking about what book series people are in, I should mention that Katie Mulligan was the heroine of the Horror Hollow series, in which she battled monstrosities that dragged their dripping, rotted feet over the bright lawns of Katie's neighborhood.

Jasper Dash had his own series too. Since the early twentieth century, back when young people's pants stopped higher up on their legs, Jasper had been knocking out aerial thieves, reclaiming diamonds, exploring abandoned mines, and getting secret codes through to Russian counts in big fur coats. He invented his own machines and vehicles and strode about, defending the American Way. He was particularly fond of strawberry-rhubarb pie.

Drgnan Pghlik was not the hero of any book except a prophesy written on birch bark and hidden in a hut high on a grassy hill. He'd never even heard of it.[*]

Brother Drgnan was training to be a Protector for the monastery of Vbngoom, but at the moment, he was staying at Jasper's house in the town of Pelt for a few weeks. He and the other kids had just gotten back from a crazy

---

[*]For the record, it foretold that a young monk from Vbngoom, the Platter of Heaven, would one day appear and overthrow the brutal dictator who ruled his homeland, Delaware, and that he would usher in a new age of plenty and joy—or would fail and plunge the Blue Hen State into a thousand years of awful tyranny.

Oh, wow. I guess that sounds kind of interesting.

But sorry, Buster McReaderson, you won't be hearing any more about that in this book.

adventure involving spies, gangsters, tigers, sentient lobsters, and giant amoebas.* Jasper was delighted to have his old friend around, and they spent hours tinkering in Jasper's laboratory, practicing their fencing, and hanging out with Lily and Katie.

This afternoon, Lily was on Drgnan Pghlik's team for their pickup game of basketball. That didn't make playing the game any easier for her. She kind of had a crush on Drgnan. She didn't want him to see her stumbling and all red and out of breath.

The thing that made it even worse that day to be tripping all over the blacktop was the game's one spectator: Katie's snobby cousin Madigan, who was visiting from New York City. Madigan sat on a bench by the side of the court, watching the whole game with hatred and trying to stifle a laugh whenever Lily fell

---

*Recounted in *Jasper Dash and the Flame-Pits of Delaware* and *Agent Q, or The Smell of Danger!*

behind or dropped the ball or stared too long at Drgnan Pghlik.

Madigan Westlake-Duvet was also in a series of books, but hers were not tales of adventure and high deeds. She was in the Snott Academy series, a stack of paperbacks with names like *2 Good 2 Be 4 Ever* and *Puppy Love Smackdown.* The stories were about bratty, beautiful kids at an exclusive New York prep school. They tricked and hurt each other and threw fits and spent most of their time looking at their own clothing in polished marble surfaces. The covers of the books just showed legs or stomachs, and sometimes teeth. That was not entirely inappropriate. The girls in the series were kind of like that.

Madigan Westlake-Duvet sat on the bench, tapping out messages on her iSquawk to her friends back in Manhattan. She was about the same age as Katie and Jasper and Lily and Drgnan, but she looked much older. She was dressed in the Snott Academy tartan skirt and a white shirt that looked like it was laundered by angels. She wore a fawn-colored tea-length Plamona overcoat and a silk scarf by Hermès. It was not easy, playing basketball near her.* Whenever she actually watched the game, she had a look of incredible, astonished boredom. Everything in her face said, *Whoa. Never. Been. So. Bored. By. Anything. In. My. Life.*

Katie caught Lily staring nervously at Madigan. "Sorry," Katie whispered. "She's visiting for the weekend. Mom said I had to bring her. I know she's kind of a snobby pain."

Lily didn't want to be rude about Katie's cousin. "Well, I bet she's really nice once you get to know her."

"No," said Katie. "I don't think anyone's really gotten to know her, or she would have been burned at the stake already."

---

*And it is not easy writing about her clothing. I have been told by the editors of the Snott Academy series to make sure I describe Madigan's outfits accurately in each scene. I don't know how I'm going to do that. I know nothing about fashion. I am wearing old, brown corduroys right now, and I think my shirt might be on backward.

"Lily!" shouted Drgnan, throwing the ball her way.

Of course, Lily was talking, so she missed it. It bounced off the court and past the bench where Madigan sat.

Flustered, Lily said, "Oh, I'm sorry—I'm sorry—I'm sorry!"

She had ignored a basketball pass from the boy she wanted most in the world to impress.

At just that instant, Madigan looked up from her iSquawk, and as Lily felt those bored and lovely eyes scrape across her, she blushed. She could feel how bad she looked in her oversize T-shirt, standing there stupidly in the middle of the court.

Drgnan waved to her and jogged over to pick up the ball. Lily knew Drgnan didn't have a crush on her. If he liked anyone in that way—I mean, *like* liked—it was Katie, who like liked him back.

Katie clearly felt bad for distracting Lily, so in a few minutes, she let Lily catch a pass. Lily dribbled it up the court. Drgnan called out, "C'mon, Lily! Good job!"

That was a great thing to hear, Drgnan calling out praise. Lily half dribbled, half ran toward the basket.

Even she knew that most of the way, she was traveling. No one said anything about it, which was worse, in a way, than someone calling her out. But anyway, this was her big moment to show she could do something for the team. A perfect layup shot . . . that was what she envisioned.

Madigan looked up.

Lily felt those awful eyes on her. Jasper flung himself in her way, grabbing at the ball.

Lily eyed the basket. She jumped!

She threw!

The ball missed the backboard completely and went bounding off into the autumn leaves.

Lily hit the earth hard. She twisted her ankle and fell.

Everyone stood awkwardly.

Katie rushed to her side. She said to everyone, "We should stop playing."

Lily protested, "Don't worry about me."

"Well," said Katie, making an excuse, "you know, it's rude of us to keep on playing with Madigan here, when she can't play."

Madigan was grinning and texting something to her New York friends.

Drgnan saw that Lily was hurt. Both her ankle and her pride. "You're right, Katie," he said. "I think we should call it a day."

Jasper, who didn't really get what was going on, said, "Call it a day? In this fine, crisp, fall air, I feel I could play until the great Sun sinks and the Pleiades come out in the heavens above us."

"No," said Katie forcefully. "We've got to hang out with Madigan."

"No prob!" called Madigan, giving a little wave. "Don't worry about me! I'm just filling the frenemies in on all the big Pelt news. Is the 'chubby' in 'chubby loser' spelled with a *y* or an *i*?"

But they did call it a day, and they all went home. As Katie and Madigan got into Mrs. Mulligan's car, Katie made a face to Lily that involved lots of teeth and furious crossed eyes. She made a *Call me* sign with her fingers. Clearly, she had things to say about spending time alone with her cousin.

Jasper and Drgnan waved heartily and climbed into Jasper's Automated Robo-Sedan, discussing chemical reactions they'd investigate at home.

And Lily, miserably, went back to her house, knowing she'd made a fool of herself.

"Good game?" said her father.

Lily shook her head sadly. She wanted to talk to her mother. She asked, "Where's Mom?"

Her father smiled. "She decided to go on a vacation."

That was weird. "It's the middle of the week," said Lily. "I just saw her like two hours ago."

"Your mom, she's been real . . . real nervous

or something," said Mr. Gefelty. "She has this weird feeling that some disaster is going to happen to her. She needed a break."

"She just left?" said Lily.

"Yeah, she'd been hyperventilating all morning. She kept calling me, worried that the ceiling was going to fall down or the whole house would be sucked into a volcanic sinkhole. Then she saw some article in the newspaper and took off."

Lily was horrified that her mother had been so worried. She felt bad for her mom. "What was the article?" she asked.

Lily's father shrugged. "I don't know. She was looking online for stuff about immortality." He stood up and walked into the kitchen. "She found some article about the town in the U.S. where the fewest people die or something. Apparently, it's famous for that. Someplace in upstate New York. She figured she'd be safe there."

Lily ran into her mother's office, which was

also their television room. Her mom's computer was still on.

"The town where the fewest people die?" said Lily. She flicked at the mouse and the screen turned on. There was an article from an old issue of the *New York Times.* The headline said,

TODBURG, N.Y., DECLARED UNDEAD CAPITAL OF THE U.S.

There was a photo of a small-town parade, with the tail end of a marching band honking on their tubas, and, ten feet behind them, a tractor pulling a bunch of girls in sparkly outfits. In between the band and the tractor, marching in broad daylight, were a bunch of transparent, bony figures dressed in the clothes of a bygone era. Ghosts. Two of the girls on the cheerleader cart were clearly dead, and had been for some time. They were zombies, green and gooey, and it looked as if they couldn't do a high kick without hurling a wet foot up into the air.

Lily stared, stunned, at the computer screen.

"Dad!" she shouted. "This isn't the town where the fewest people *die*! It's a town *of the undead!*"

"That's what I said," he called in. "The undead. People who haven't died."

"The undead," said Lily, "*have* died! They've come *back from the dead!* Like vampires and ghosts and ghouls!"

Mr. Gefelty sighed. "Honey, listen to the words. *Undead* means 'not dead.'"

"No, it doesn't! 'Undead' means the walking dead!"

"The prefix *un* doesn't mean someone's walking. For example, just because you're being *unreasonable* doesn't mean you're being *the walking reasonable.*"

"Don't you see?" Lily said, breathless. "Something terrible is going to happen!"

More than that, Lily realized: Her mom's

attempt to save herself from disaster was the very thing that was leading her toward disaster—in the most ghostly, ghoulish, vampiric, zombified town in America!

3

Lily Gefelty's mother drove along a lonely highway through the rainy night. The trees were black against the spitting, grumbling sky.

No one was in the other lanes. Her car whirred along, alone.

Mrs. Gefelty gripped the wheel anxiously and kept looking in her rearview mirror. She had a strong feeling disaster was about to strike. The kind of disaster that always overtook mothers in novels for the young. It hung over her like an anvil on a fraying rope. But in this case, she didn't know what direction disaster would come from. She watched the woods carefully, squinting into the pines.

She did not realize that up ahead, a bridge

was out because of the rain. And she did not realize that a truck, trying to avoid the fallen bridge, had skidded and crashed, right across the road.

And she did not realize that at the last rest stop, when she'd gotten out of the car to buy an energy drink from a machine, an Adirondack tarantula—very deadly, very rare—had clambered into her car and was, at that very moment, slinking toward her ankles under the seat.

Unknowing, she pressed the accelerator with her foot. The hulking spider, bristling with coarse hairs, watched her ankle shift.

Mrs. Gefelty sniffled. She had picked up a cold in the chilly autumn rain. She was trying to convince herself that it was not a deadly disease in disguise. She told herself that very few deadly diseases start with a runny nose.

She sniffled again. She twitched her nose.

(Down below her, the tarantula twitched the furry fingerlings on either side of his mouth.)

"But what if I *do* have a deadly disease?"

she asked out loud. "No. I'm being ridiculous. . . . It's just a cold. . . . But what if I do? Or even worse, what if it *is* just a cold but I go into the hospital for a test—and *ironically I catch a deadly disease from another patient in the hospital?*" Though she knew this was not very likely, still, it consumed her. "Then . . . ," she whispered, "then Lily and Ben will be all alone. . . . And if it's anything like all those dead mother books, Lily will become a pickpocket or a shoplifter . . . or she'll have to get a pet raccoon to teach her the meaning of trust. . . ."

These awful thoughts only made Mrs. Gefelty sniffle more.

So she reached under the seat for her box of Kleenex. Which was right next to the tarantula.

I should take this moment to explain that tarantulas are usually not particularly dangerous to humans. They are one of the spiders that have gotten a bad reputation because they are big and ugly. Sure, spy movies always have villains releasing tarantulas in people's hotel rooms. If you're a spy, tarantulas are as common in seaside resort bedrooms as free body wash. But they are not deadly.

So, spies of the world, relax. Light a few scented candles and lie back in your tubs, deep in the suds. Smoke your cigars while the tarantulas scuttle to and fro along the rim of the tub, doing eight-legged push-ups on your complimentary soap. While you soak, let the tarantulas rush about in their formations like synchronized swimmers in an old Esther Williams movie, toppling into the water one by one and waving their little arms. You will be fine.

Unless they are Adirondack tarantulas. Those are absolutely deadly. One bite can kill a person. Then you're not just in the tub—you're in hot water. *Boiling* hot water.

Mrs. Gefelty reached under the seat for another tissue.

4

Lily's mother fumbled for the box of Kleenex. Her hand, fingers spread wide, matched the movements of the tarantula, as if spider and hand were about to do a love scene in a ballet. Then Mrs. Gefelty found the box. She tugged at the tissue. The tarantula crept closer, spreading its fangs.

The tissue wouldn't come free. She kept tugging.

The tarantula softly, softly, softly touched the juicy part of her palm. He prepared to bite. . . . And, raising his forelegs—

A TRUCK! ACROSS THE ROAD!

Mrs. Gefelty spun the wheel wildly. Her car skidded!

The tarantula was thrown back! Tumbling

out behind the front seat into the backseat!

The car came to a stop.

An eighteen-wheeler had lost control in the drizzle and was jackknifed across the road.

As I mentioned a few pages ago.

Oh, Mrs. Gefelty, how I wish I could tell you of other dangers that lurk around you. But here I am, just an author, hovering helplessly like a ghost outside a window.

"That was a close call," whispered Mrs. Gefelty. She blinked, and felt the zing of adrenaline up and down her arms. She looked out into the dark night.

It was a particularly close call, she realized. If the truck had not been crashed across the road, its headlights would not have been shining right on the fallen bridge, and she might have driven straight ahead off a cliff.

She opened the car door and stepped out.

She looked around. The truck driver was nowhere to be seen.

There was a teenage boy, however, standing

in the rain. He was very, very pale and wore a hoodie.

"Is everyone okay?" Mrs. Gefelty called to the boy.

The boy nodded slowly. His pale eyes watched her.

"Are you looking for a ride?" she asked him.

He nodded again.

She walked over to the chasm where the bridge had led over a river. "Sorry," she said. "I can't go anywhere either, with this bridge down."

The rain was getting heavier. Mrs. Gefelty held her hand over her eyes to look at the boy.

He pointed into the woods.

Mrs. Gefelty saw that there was a rutted dirt road that led into the dark forest.

"Oh!" said Mrs. Gefelty. "Is that a detour?"

The boy nodded.

"Well, that's awesome!" she said, hoping that the word "awesome" made her seem friendly and cool to the teenager. She opened the passenger door. "You're soaking wet.

Here, get in and I'll give you a ride."

The pale, pale boy got into the car. He sat, staring straight ahead.

Mrs. Gefelty got in, shut the door, smiled widely at the boy, sneezed, and backed up. She headed the car into the woods. It jounced and bounced over ruts and roots.

Meanwhile, behind her, in the crashed truck, the driver crouched low, rubbing himself with garlic. There was no way he was getting out of the cab of the truck until the sun was up, that was for darn tootin'.

His truck had obscured the sign alongside the highway, so Mrs. Gefelty had not been able to read:

EXIT 36
TODBURG, N.Y.
Welcome to Todburg!

Established 1821
Population: -1,200

"A Town You'll Never Leave!"

5

"I'm worried about my mom," Lily whispered on the phone to Katie. "I mean, I'm sorry to bother you when your cousin's there, but—"

"No probs," said Katie. "Madigan's baking her fingernails in a special infrared oven." Lily could almost hear Katie rolling her eyes. Katie continued, "Listen, Lily, where was it you said your mom went?"

"It's called Todburg. It's in upstate New York."

Katie inhaled sharply. "Todburg? Lily, that's really bad. Really, really. Todburg is one of the only places in America that's supposed to be *more haunted than Horror Hollow.*"

Now Lily was *very* worried. When she got

off the phone with Katie, she went downstairs to talk to her dad. Needless to say, he didn't believe her.

"That's ridiculous, Lily," said her father.

"Katie knows what she's talking about. She's fought off a bunch of zombies and stuff."

"Look," said Mr. Gefelty, dialing his phone. "Let's call your mother. Okay? Will that help?" He held the phone up to his ear, crunched between his shoulder and his head. "It is the modern world, after all."

Lily could hear her mother's phone ring. She could hear her mother pick it up and say, "Hello."

Mr. Gefelty said, "Hey there, Suze. Lily was concerned. We just wanted to check to see you're okay. How are things going? . . . Uh-huh . . . Yuh . . . Yuh . . . Yuh . . . Oh, whoa. . . . Wow! . . . Uh-huh . . . Yuh . . . Yuh . . . All righty, then. That's great. . . . Talk to you later. . . . Love you!" He hung up.

"She's fine," he told Lily. "Everything's

great. The bridge was out because of the rain, but she didn't go off the cliff because the head-lights from a truck that got in an accident were shining on the twisted girders. Now she's riding on a dirt road through the woods in a thunderstorm with a pale, pale kid she picked up near the wreck of the truck. She says she'll be in Todburg in a few minutes. So. There it is. Everything's fine. Crisis averted."

Somehow, Lily didn't feel so good about things.

6

The rain was pouring down, beating on the roof of the car.

"You're lucky you're not out in this," Mrs. Gefelty said to her pale passenger. "You'd catch your death."

He rolled his white, slack-mouthed face toward her and surveyed her with his unblinking eyes.

She leaned toward the misty windshield and flicked the headlights from high beams to low beams to high beams again. Nothing really could penetrate the rain and the fog in the forest. The car bumped and jolted along the track. The windshield wipers beat frantically back and forth. Rough tree trunks floated up out of the dark and passed them on each side like a procession of corpses.

Mrs. Gefelty said, "You know, I came up here because I've had this premonition that something really bad was going to happen to me. But maybe that was it, that was the disaster back there—that bridge. It's weird. I seem to actually be having really good luck tonight! For example, I'm so glad I ran into you and you knew this shortcut. This'll take us right into downtown Todburg, huh?"

The teen nodded.

"That's great," said Mrs. Gefelty. She sneezed. "Sorry," she said. "I have a little cold. Hope you don't catch it!" The kid said nothing. Mrs. Gefelty tried, "You know, I have a daughter who's just a few years younger than you."

She did not know that the boy was actually ninety-six years old.

The car veered and slid in the mud.

Mrs. Gefelty sneezed again, this time very hard.

The boy had started smacking his lips weirdly. His fangs glinted in the blue lights from the dashboard.

"This forest is kind of creepy, isn't it?" said Mrs. Gefelty. "Maybe this isn't a great detour."

The boy prepared himself to bite her neck. He raised his hands. His fingers were webbed like a bat's wings.

And when Mrs. Gefelty was concentrating on the bumpy road, he leaped to suck her blood.

At the same moment, Mrs. Gefelty sneezed, doubling over.

When she sat back, she realized she had scrunched the boy's head behind her shoulders. His teeth somehow had gotten tangled in her seat belt.

"How did you manage to do that?" she said. She helped him unhook himself from the retractable belt.

He sat back. He watched her carefully.

She swerved around huge puddles.

The boy was hungry for blood. He'd been frustrated by the truck driver, who, after the crash, had locked his doors and hadn't let the boy in. But now, here was this lady. It was a perfect opportunity. He prepared himself for the kill. The boy made slurping noises and tickled the air with his webbed fingers.

Again, he lunged.

And as he lunged, Mrs. Gefelty reached under her seat for the Kleenex.

They slammed heads.

"Oh! Wow! I'm sorry! I'm so sorry!" she said. "I was trying to get a tissue. I didn't mean to head-butt you. Your nose is bleeding!"

The boy snuffled. He tried to look at his own nose. His pale eyes crossed.

Mrs. Gefelty said, "Here. Do you want one? A tissue?"

She held one out for the boy.

He stared at her neck.

"Go on," she said. "They're infused with aloe lotion. For added soothing action. Tip your head back. I'm a mother. I know these things. Come on. Tip your head back."

The vampire boy snortled.

"Now here. Take this. Press it to your nose."

She was holding the tissue out to him when she sneezed again, violently. Her hand whacked the kid right in the face.

"Oh! Whoa! I'm sorry again! Oh my gosh, look at your poor nose! That made it even worse!"

The boy rasped, "Blood . . . Blood."

"Let me get you another tissue."

Staring into the darkness, she fumbled under the seat.

"Here," she said. "Take the whole box."

She handed him the box of Kleenex. With an angry Adirondack tarantula sitting on top, waiting to strike.

The vampire boy made a meeping noise.

The tarantula growled.

Mrs. Gefelty didn't see any of it. She swerved the car through the woods.

Now, any horror-novel naturalist will tell you that the bat and the tarantula are natural enemies. And any certified camp counselor will tell you that a bat and a vampire are basically the same animal. So the spider and the undead boy stared at each other in eternal, vicious hatred.

That's right: vampires vs. tarantulas.

The way the world should be.

The spider leaped.

Fanged boy and hairy, eight-legged pest struggled in the seat, both of them squealing, and Mrs. Gefelty said, "What's going on over—" and then turned her head and looked—saw the awful spider—and she shrieked—and pointed—and the car shot off the path into the woods.

Screaming, Mrs. Gefelty steered a crazy course through trees, over bracken, under brush—while the boy and the spider kept up their fight to the death.

Until Mrs. Gefelty sneezed again. And the steering wheel jerked to the right.

And the car rolled over a steep hillside.

It rolled many times, bouncing against trees like a pinball against the bumpers.

Its headlights flashed through the heavens, down to the earth.

It slid, upside down, down the slope.

Mrs. Gefelty, the boy, and the spider watched the world twirl and thump heavily around them. They were nothing but a mess of elbows and knees.*

Bam! Boom! Bash!

Down the hill.

Until the car slid out onto a paved street at the bottom.

The car was totaled.

It lay upside down in the middle of a road. It had faint white moth wings of broken glass spread on each side of it.

---

*Remember that the average number of knees for passengers in this car was unusually high because of the spider. 2 human knees + 2 vampire knees + 8 tarantula knees = 12 knees, divided by 3 passengers = an average of 4 knees per passenger.

The rain fell more softly now. Up the street, there were old nineteenth-century storefronts made of brick and plate glass. There were streetlamps. The fog drifted down the slope from the dark, tangled wood.

Mrs. Gefelty forced her door open and staggered out.

"Oh my gosh. Oh my gosh," she said, looking at all the damage. "Where did that spider go?"

The vampire boy crawled out of his flattened door. His nose was still bleeding, and he was covered in bruises and poisonous spider bites that would have killed a normal person.

Mrs. Gefelty rushed toward him. "Are you okay?" she asked. "Really? Are you okay?"

The vampire backed away from her in self-protective terror. She had bashed him, bruised him, bloodied him, and sicced a tarantula on him. He couldn't take any more.

"You could have been killed!" Mrs. Gefelty exclaimed. "I'm so sorry!"

He held up his webbed hands and motioned for her to keep her distance.

"Let me find the first-aid kit in the car!"

He shook his head frantically. He clearly didn't want to be anywhere near her.

"Ow!" she exclaimed, grabbing at her head. "I really think I hurt my neck. Could you take a look at it? Right here? Would you just check it out, close up, and see if anything's . . . Hey! Where are you going? Hey!"

The vampire boy, terrified of her, had started running, tripped, fallen, half risen, turned into a bat, and was flying away. The spider crawled out of the wreck and scuttled along the pavement in hot pursuit.

In disbelief, Mrs. Gefelty watched the bat-boy fly away.

"I must have hit my head," she concluded. "Yeah."

She looked at Todburg's Main Street: the storefronts, mostly empty of business. The lights casting cones of rain. The huge Victorian

Gothic hotel that looked like no one had stayed in it for many years.

"Well, my car's wrecked and there's a driving rainstorm," she said, "so I guess I'll have to stay overnight at that creepy old hotel. Oh well." She pried open the crushed trunk, got out her suitcase, and headed up the stone steps.

She stopped before the ornate front door. "Here goes," she said. "How bad can a weird hotel be, after what I've been through?"

Those, as it turned out, were the last words the living Mrs. Gefelty would speak in this book.

Lightning crashed in the sky.

She opened the hotel door and went inside.

7

It was two days later. Lily had invited her friends over to her house to discuss what she should do about her mother. She and her father hadn't heard from Mrs. Gefelty since the night of the rainstorm. It was time to make a plan.

The problem was that they couldn't openly talk about the problem with Madigan Westlake-Duvet around. She didn't believe in ghosts, ghouls, or zombies. When she overheard them discussing the undead armies of Todburg, she thought they were "pretending."

Katie took a moment when Madigan went outside to get better reception for her iSquawk to say, "Okay. Here's the thing. If we have to go to Todburg to search for Lily's mom, I won't be allowed to go unless Madigan goes. My mom won't let me. And Madigan won't go unless she thinks going to Todburg's cool. So we need to make up some special code words. For example, instead of 'incredible danger,' we'll say, 'sunny beaches.' And instead of 'the ravenous undead,' we'll say, 'Hollywood movie stars.' And instead of 'certain death,' we'll say, 'high-end celebrity makeovers.'"

They all looked anxiously at each other. Jasper said, "Why, this is a fine fix, pals."

Brother Drgnan Pghlik agreed, "It is a dark day when the dead walk again."

"Yeah," said Katie. "You mean Hollywood movie stars. It is a dark day when Hollywood movie stars walk again."

Lily wondered why she and her friends all cared so much what Madigan thought. This was an urgent situation. But even she didn't want to look lame in front of the New Yorker.

"Before she returns," said Jasper, "I should remind you all that if we do need to travel to upstate New York, we can no longer use the Gyroscopic Sky-Suite. It crashed in Dover, Delaware, as you know. We can, however, take my Astounding Automated Robo-Sedan. It will be difficult to seat us all, because it only seats four, and the robot takes up one seat. But surely, to save Lily's mother, no one will mind."

Madigan swayed into the room on a pair of kitten-heel slides by Me-*ow!* of Tokyo; her voile halter maxidress by Uxury swished around her. She looked angry and bored at the same time, which was not easy.

"Oh. My. Gosh," she said. "Hello? My friend Jared says he's going to quit the lacrosse team because he can't stand to be on it after Tip Drake stole Nola from him. What is Snott lax going to do without Jared?"

No one else in the room had any idea who these people were.

Katie smiled pleasantly at her cousin. "We were just talking about taking a little trip."

Madigan stared at her with eyes full of baleful disdain.

Katie continued, "We're thinking of going to Todburg, New York. Enjoying the sunny beaches."

"Yes," said Jasper woodenly. (He was not very good at lying.) "There is much, much . . . sunny beach there."

"Where is Todburg?"

"Up north," Katie answered.

"Okay," whispered Madigan, as if to herself. "At least no one important will see me there."

"We . . . ," said Lily hesitantly, "we need to make a plan. In case my mother has been taken . . . by all the Hollywood movie stars there to a . . . a party. We have to figure out how to crash the party."

"Just get your goddess on and walk in the front door," Madigan suggested. "Unless you're low on goddess."

Lily said, "It is very hard to stop, um, movie stars. Because they are already—"

"They eat brains!" Jasper exclaimed, unable to help himself. "And there is no organ I treasure more!"

"Except," said Drgnan quietly, "the heart." He patted his own.

Katie sighed dreamily. "That's a beautiful thing to say."

"What I mean," said Lily, "was that the thing that makes, um, movie stars particularly . . . beachy . . . is that they're already . . . you know . . . asleep, sunbathing . . . so it's hard to . . . put them to sleep again."

"Oh, don't worry, honey," said Madigan. "Just keep talking. You'll manage."

"She didn't mean asleep," Katie intervened. "She meant high-end celebrity makeovers. Right, Lily? High-end celebrity makeovers?"

"Yeah," said Lily uncertainly. She had forgotten that "high-end celebrity makeovers" stood for "certain death."

"You mean," said Katie, "how will we make

sure that the movie stars get high-end celebrity makeovers."

"Holy water!" said Drgnan.

"You *mean*," said Katie, "mango spritzer." She explained to Madigan, "Drgnan meant mango spritzer. Like flavored seltzer water. Not holy water."

Jasper's eyes suddenly were wide with excitement. "A spritzer gun! A gun that shoots holy wa—spritzer at the enemy!"

He and Drgnan were practically shivering with the thrill of it. A holy water squirt gun. By George, this was how a day was supposed to begin! Drgnan aimed an imaginary gun at imaginary zombies, squinted down the bar-rel, and made squelchy sounds as he picked his opponents off.

"We'll get right on it," said Jasper. "We can build one in my lab. It will take us but a quick lick of time."

"Um," said Madigan, "I'm not sure that when the glamorami talk about 'high-end celebrity makeovers,' they mean being sprayed in the face with seltzer water by a boy in a dress and a bottom-drawer loser dressed like an old-timey margarine commercial."

Drgnan and Jasper looked embarrassed, although even this could not dampen their enthusiasm for high-intensity holy water squirt guns.

"Then the other thing we have to think about," said Lily, "if we're going to avoid, um, high-end celebrity makeovers ourselves is that—"

At that moment, the front door slammed open. Thank goodness, because I can't stand this code talk anymore. So, yes, the front door slammed open and someone walked into the house.

"I'm home!" sang out Mrs. Gefelty's voice.

The kids looked at each other, astonished.

Lily and her friends ran to the door.

There was Lily's mother, smelling of the fresh autumn air, her coat swirling around her.

Mr. Gefelty went to give her a peck on the cheek. She threw her arms around him. She exclaimed, "It was absolutely marvelous, darling. Marvelous! I feel renewed." She held her hand out in front of her and wriggled her fingers. "It's so wonderful! My anxiety is gone. I have learned to feel again."

Then she saw the kids, and a big, bright smile crossed her face. *"Darling!"* she cried. "Darling Lily! Mommy is sorry she had to go away! But she's back! She's back!"

Mrs. Gefelty swooped in for a big hug.

Lily watched her mom.

"Mom," said Lily. "Mom . . . that's Katie's cousin Madigan. I'm over here."

Mrs. Gefelty looked up, a little embarrassed, from Madigan's shoulder.

She had not known her own daughter.

8

The autumn rain fell outside the house in the November darkness. It made all the shadows of hulking things outside look uneven. No angle was straight. All houses were crooked houses. All trees were twisted trees.

And inside, at the dinner table, the Gefelty family did not seem like the Gefelty family.

It might not have been clear to an outsider. Mrs. Gefelty talked loudly and howled with laughter throughout the meal. But that in itself was what made Lily afraid. Her mother was not a particularly loud woman.

Up until now. "Todburg is an absolutely charming little resort town. You must, *must* go too. We can make it a family outing! Oh, there's a little museum, and a hardware store, and a feed store, and some boutiques, and sunny beaches. . . . Plenty of sunny beaches. Who *made* these little rolls? It is *such* a pleasure to nibble on a little roll like this again. . . . Oh, the car crash. The car crash! We rolled down an iddle-widdle hill. An ickle-wickle baby hill. Well, the automobile was destroyed. My, oh my, was it ever!" She swung her hands around widely as she talked. "Ka-BLOOM! So . . . No way for me to drive it home. It was squashed like a pancake. So I *rented* a car. On my *credit card!* It was such a pleasure to drive. You can see it out there in the driveway. Ben, I love that car. Do you know, it has the most marvelous thing: It is *automatic.* I mean, it *switches gears by itself!* So you don't have to switch gears with a gearshift!" Mrs. Gefelty clapped her hands together. "I can't tell you how delightful that is. It frees one hand for ventriloquism." She made her right hand a puppet and it sang, "It's delightful! It's delicious! It's *de-lovely*!"

Lily looked carefully at her mother. She wasn't sure, but she thought that cars with automatic transmissions had been around for a long time, about fifty years or something. In fact, she was pretty sure that her mom's own car—the one that lay somewhere in Todburg, upside down—was an automatic.

So why didn't her mother seem to remember that—or anything else?

And then it struck her: amnesia. Her mother must have hit her head in the fall down the hill. And now, though she didn't realize it, she had forgotten half of what she knew.

Her whole personality was different.

"Lily," said her mother. "Lils. Can I call you Lils? Between girls—Ben, shut your ears, this is hen chatter—Lils, do we have to have a little discussion?"

"I don't . . . I don't know, Mom."

"Oh, come now, come now! I am your mother! I know you! I saw how you looked at that darling little monk boy. Do you have a crush? Do you have a little crush? Because he is a *very handsome* young man."

Lily blushed. She couldn't believe her mother was saying these things. They never talked about stuff like this in her family. What she'd learned in school that day, sure. What they'd heard from Uncle Michael, yes. Making guesses about the fastest speeds a kangaroo could hop, certainly. But whether Drgnan was a very handsome young man, no.

Lily didn't know what to say.

Her mother certainly did. "Hush! Hush, my darling! Your heart is still little, but that doesn't stop it from breaking! Oh, *l'amour! L'amour!*" she cried in French. Lily took Spanish in school, but she knew enough French to know that "amour" meant "love," and to know that her mother's French accent was terrible. Or at least it was terrible right now, at this dinner. But in fact, her mother had spent a year in Paris when she was in college, and supposedly spoke French really well.

Lily mumbled, "Can I be excused?"

"But darling child, what are you going to *do* about the boy? What are you going to do?"

Lily hesitated. "The dishes," she answered. She collected the plates, took them into the kitchen, and washed them.

She could hear her parents in the dining room giggling and kissing. It made her very uncomfortable. Her mother kept joyfully exclaiming, *"L'amour!"* in her new, terrible accent.

But it sounded more like she was saying, *"La mort! La mort!"*

Which, in French, means *"death."*

9

Amnesia, said Lily to herself as she brushed her teeth. *She has amnesia.*

Lily scrubbed her molars. She spat out toothpaste. She brushed again.

That's all it is, Lily thought. *Amnesia. Tomorrow she'll go to the doctor. Then she'll be fine.*

Lily spat again. She was done. She stuck her toothbrush in the stand, wiped her mouth, and went out into the hallway.

Her father was next in line.

"Dad," Lily whispered. "Mom's different."

"I know," he said, beaming. "It's great."

"No, I mean she doesn't seem to remember anything." Lily said very, very softly, "I think she has amnesia."

Her father looked at her in a long-suffering way. He rolled his eyes. "Amnesia?" he said. "You get the craziest ideas, honey-bear."

"She seems like a different person."

"Because, honey, sometimes when people go away for a little vacation, a little TLC, they come back *feeling like different people*. That's all it is. She seems like a different person because she feels like a different person. Happier. More alive. That's the best way of putting it: more alive. It's great to have her back."

Lily couldn't even look him in the face. He was lying to himself, and he knew it.

She went to bed.

The rain fell on the neighborhood. It fell on the dead leaves in the gutters.

It poured down on the silent cars in the driveways.

Lily lay in bed listening.

She couldn't sleep.

Sometime around two in the morning, she

got up. She didn't know why. She just had a funny feeling.

She walked down the hallway. She went to her parents' door to peek in. She opened the door.

The room was dark. Her father lay curled up, facing toward the window, breathing softly.

Her mother was floating several inches above the bed.

Lily gasped. Her mother's eyes were closed and her breath was regular. But she hovered, motionless, on her back. Her hair was spread out around her head and moved gently, touched by sparks of green. A green negative of her body, blurred like a badly shot photo, hovered around her limbs.

Her father lay next to this glowing monster.

Whatever this was, it was not her mother.

Lily wondered whether she should scream. Wake him up. Show him what was floating next to him.

She stared, aghast. Absently, she twisted the doorknob in her hand.

She opened her mouth to say something.

And the creature's head snapped up. The eyes opened: two pits of green light.

The thing stared at her. That was all. Just stared at her, as if to say, *I know you have seen this. But you will say nothing.*

As if to say, *Back away. Go back to your room, little girl. There's nothing you can do. Nothing.*

The creature reached out a hand and laid it on Mr. Gefelty's sleeping shoulder. He murmured pleasantly and patted it, turned over, went back to sleep.

The creature did not frown or smile. It kept its eyes on Lily.

Lily backed out of the room.

She went to bed.

In the morning, Mrs. Gefelty made a batch of her special pancakes.

She called them her "special pancakes," but she had never ever made them before.

10

The morning rain was beading on the huge plate-glass windows of Jasper Dash's hyper-modern home of the future when the telephone rang. He was drinking his morning glass of Gargletine Brand Breakfast Drink™, which keeps your skin and hair shiny all through the day; Drgnan was eating a bowl of bulrushes. (Monks are not allowed to eat anything that tastes good.) Jasper got the phone. "It's Lily!" he announced. "Why, Lily, it is tremendous that you called. While it's swell that your mother came home yesterday, Drgnan and I were a little disappointed that we wouldn't have a chance to build high-power holy water squirt guns. So last night we decided we'd have a go at it anyway. After a great deal of tinkering and a fair amount of electrical discharge from lasery sorts of machines, we believe we have come up with a device that can be filled at a garden hose—but that actually blesses the water before spraying it at undead enemies. If Katie should ever need—" Jasper yelped.

"Jasper?" said Lily's voice.

"Ack! Drgnan is squirting me as we speak— He is—here he is!"

There was a scuffle, and Drgnan grabbed the phone out of Jasper's hand. Jasper pulled down his flight goggles and looked steely. He crossed his arms.

"Morning greets you, Lily," said Drgnan. "The rain showers have fallen on Jasper. Inside the house."

"So you two invented a holy water squirt gun?"

"Yes. And it is in excellent working condition."

"It could still come in useful," whispered Lily.

Drgnan heard something in Lily's voice. He waved for Jasper to stop preparing a counter-attack. Jasper stalled and backed off, dropping his hands.

Through the phone, Lily said softly, "Things are really wrong. I mean really, really wrong. We have to go up there to Todburg right away and find out what happened to my mother." She paused, and with a catch in her voice, said, "My real mother."

Immediately, Drgnan realized what this meant. "Oh, Lily," said Drgnan. "Oh, Lily, Lily." His voice was thick with compassion. "Who is the mother who is there at the house?"

"I don't know," whispered Lily, almost blubbering. "That's what we have to find out."

"Just give Jasper and me a few minutes and we'll be over in the Robo-Sedan. Do not fear, Lily. By Saint Grdplex, your friends are with you."

He said good-bye and hung up.

Jasper looked grim. He could tell what Lily and Drgnan had been talking about.

"The gun," he said, "may come in useful?"

Drgnan nodded.

"That is rotten."

"She wishes us to go with her to Todburg, the most undead-infested town in America, and seek answers there."

Jasper nodded. He lifted the flight goggles off his eyes and rubbed at the rings they left. "We're off," he said. "Pack your things, Drg."

Jasper's mother was leaning against the kitchen counter, looking at him sadly. "Where are you going to now?" she asked.

"Upstate New York!" he exclaimed. "To conquer the undead!" He held up his glass of sludgy Gargletine.

She shook her head. She turned and began to fold the dishrags into neat, pressed squares.

Everyone arrived at Lily's house an hour later, ready to go to Todburg. They sat in her living room, planning things.

Madigan was using her iSquawk to tell her BFFs that she was off to some town where supposedly a lot of Hollywood movie stars hung out. She actually thought it was stupid, because her dorky cousin Katie had suggested it, but she described it to her New York friends in a way that made it sound totally cool, like it had been her idea, and probably by the end of the day, she'd be hanging out on the sunny beaches of Todburg with Carlton Brunk, teen hunk, star of such movies as *Go for Broke*, and *Hold My Face*, and last year's rollicking comedy *Smooch Zoo*.

"It will take us a long time to get there," said Jasper. "It is quite far away."

"How are we going to find out about what happened to Mrs. Gefelty when—"

The door slammed open. The fake Mrs. Gefelty was standing there in a red dress. She had something hidden behind her back in one of her hands. Everyone exchanged glances.

"Did I hear my name?" she asked, smiling. She walked in. "Lily," she said. "Lils. I have the grandest idea. Why don't you kids play a little round of . . ." She pulled out from behind her, with a great deal of flourish—an empty Coke bottle. She murmured, "Spin. The. Bottle."

She put it down in the middle of all of them, gave it a spin, then stood. She winked hideously, pointed (awfully) right at Drgnan Pghlik, and jerked her head to signal to Lily that *Okay, this is your big opportunity.*

Katie, thankfully, did not see the wink. Drgnan saw the wink. Madigan saw the wink. Jasper saw the wink and had no idea what was going on. Lily saw the wink, and crinkled up like paper inside.

Both she and Drgnan blushed deeply. Drgnan lifted the flap on the bottom of the sofa cover, as if there might be something really interesting there that rolled under sofas.

"What about it, kids?" said Mrs. Gefelty.

"Whoa," said Madigan. "I think I just got whiplash from being jerked back to 1952."

"Mom," said Lily, "that's okay. That's . . . All

right, maybe! Thanks! Oh, I'm going to Jasper's for the night. You don't have to drive me. We'll take his Robo-Sedan. Is that okay? Can I, um, stay over there?"

"You," said Mrs. Gefelty, kissing her on the forehead, "are my beautiful, wonderful daughter, and you can do anything you put your mind to."

With this completely embarrassing reply, she winked at everyone, kicked up her heel, and sauntered out of the living room.

There was a silence for a while.

"Well," said Madigan. "That was really awkward."

Katie looked around, confused.

"Shall we go?" said Jasper. "There is no profit in dawdling."

They walked out of the house.

"That's not my mother," Lily whispered to Katie. "That's not her."

"I know," said Katie. She patted her friend's arm. "We're going to find her."

Katie did not say it, but they both knew that she was thinking, *If your mother is still alive.*

A few minutes later, they were cruising away from the town of Pelt, crammed in the Robo-Sedan, headed for the undead capital of America.

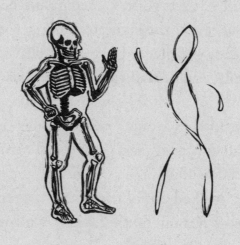

11

It was a long, uncomfortable trip with the five of them shoved into seats made for three. Katie was crammed in next to Drgnan Pghlik and didn't seem to mind it much. ("Don't worry about me! My arm hurts, but it will be okay. What's important is that Madigan doesn't feel scrunched.")

Madigan did feel scrunched, clearly, and wore a look of chilly hatred on her face for the whole several hundred miles' drive. She was next to Lily, folded up like a stainless-steel wine rack. She was furious that all the scrunching might wrinkle her La Mona skirt and her bone white pleated-front blouse by Félix. She wore Bob Obi sunglasses and a pair of Mooch Couture clamdiggers on her feet.

"Well," she said, "at least I'll die of asphyxiation before I die of boredom."

"A little dull?" said Jasper. "Then we can put on my radiophonic—"

I'm sorry. Excuse me. Someone who just came into the room and read the last few paragraphs over my shoulder has informed me that "Mooch Couture clamdiggers" are pants, not shoes, so Madigan should not be wearing them on her feet. If she wore them on her feet, they would be a very long, wrinkled, bedraggled kind of footwear.

I'm sorry. It has to be admitted, when it comes to fashion, I know absolutely nothing. So I need to back up a few lines and do a little substitution.

The guy who's reading over my shoulder just suggested, "You know what you need to have her wearing? Some crushed-berry Manolo Blahnik flats," which I found very informative, so I followed it up by asking him other questions of interest, such as who he was, and what he was doing in my apartment.

"Oh. Yeah," he explained, pointing at himself. "Robber. Robbing."

I nodded. "I don't know how much I've got for you. My stereo is pretty old. My computer is covered in microwave popcorn husks. I don't keep any cash around the house."

He snorted. "And we know there isn't going to be anything worth taking in your clothes closet."

"All right! All right!" I growled. "Let's make this quick. What are you looking for?"

"Gems?"

"Here's a box of bulldog clips and a coupon for a free entrée at J. P. Barnigan's American Family Restaurants. Let's call it even."

He nodded gruffly, waved, and climbed out the window.

So, that little episode resolved, I now turn back to my story.

Madigan was furious that all the scrunching

might wrinkle her La Mona skirt and bone white pleated-front blouse by Félix. She wore Bob Obi sunglasses and a pair of crushed-berry Manolo Blahnik flats on her feet.

"My name is Doug," said the robber, sticking his head through the window. "In case you're interested."

"Great to meet you," I said.

"Aren't you going to tell me your name?"

"It's on the mailbox in the front hall."

"All righty. If that's how you want to be. It looks like you're busy. Check you later."

"Careful," I said. "I'm on the fourth floor."

"You aren't kidding about that," he chuckled, and disappeared.

I now have shut the window and locked it.

So let's really get back to the story.

Oh, who cares about the car ride? It's an Astounding Robo-Sedan! It must be able to fly.

Go ahead, young Dash—order your robot to open up the rocket thrusters! You know you can't resist anything with rocket thrusters.

And so the car shoots along the highway as minivans and pickups fall far behind it. . . . Miles of interstate highway scream beneath the wheels. . . . Church steeples go shooting past like pickets on a fence. Albany is just a blur. And then the landscape falls away beneath them—they're flying—soaring above the gentle fields of upstate New York.

And a scarce half an hour later, they're coming down on the main street of Todburg, right next to the crumpled wreck of Mrs. Gefelty's car.

12

Stepping out of the steaming Robo-Sedan in her La Mona skirt and stylish Manolo Blahnik flats, Madigan looked around the center of Todburg with disgust. "This is *it*?" she said. "I thought it was supposed to be *fabulous*. Where are the movie stars? The only people here are hiding inside their houses and looking out their windows."

"Well," said Katie, "you're always saying it's more important to be seen than to see."

"What I say," said Madigan irritably, "is that the best thing is to be seen with the see-and-be-seen crowd. Which doesn't include people hiding in upstairs rooms"—(she pointed)—"lighting welding torches."

Drgnan said grimly, "They must be preparing for nightfall."

"Are you telling me that's what the club scene is going to be like here? Old guys with flamethrowers?"

Drgnan and Jasper exchanged puzzled looks.

Jasper went to pull his high-pressure holy water squirt gun out of the trunk.

Lily, shutting the car door behind her, looked slowly around Main Street. So this was where her mother had disappeared. Somewhere in these old storefronts was the secret to what had happened.

Lily gestured toward the old, rotting Victorian place by the side of the road. "That's the hotel where she said she stayed," Lily explained. "Let's go in there and get a couple of rooms for the night. We can ask if they saw my mom."

They went in with their suitcases and backpacks. An older man was behind the desk. He wore a plaid vest with a zipper. "Sure," he said when they asked. "There was a lady came through here the other day. Stayed a couple of nights. Really enjoyed the place. Went out on the town."

"Do you know what she did?" Lily asked. "Where she went or anything?"

"Well, no, but there's, uh . . ." The man looked around the hall carefully. He leaned over the desk. He explained, "It's not a great idea to go out on the streets at night. It becomes kind of a different town at night."

Jasper asked, "Because of gambling dens and the juke joints that play honky-tonk music?"

The hotel proprietor gave Jasper an odd look. "No . . . I can't say it's really because of, ahhhh, honky-tonk music. It's more . . ."

"The walking legions of the undead?" Drgnan suggested.

The hotel proprietor nodded and tapped his nose, as if to say, *Yup. On the nose.*

The kids went up to their rooms. The girls were in one and the boys were in the other, across the hall.

Lily was anxious. She stared out the window at the street below.

"Don't worry, Lily," said Katie. "We're here now. We'll find a clue."

"A clue to *what*?" asked Madigan. She looked furiously at the two girls. "Spill it! I know you're hiding something from me. You get all cute and winky whenever you talk about the sunny beaches and the high-end celebrity makeovers. So come on. What are we really doing here?"

Lily couldn't bring herself to tell Madigan why they'd come to Todburg. She was sure that no girl from Snott Academy had ever had her mother replaced by the undead.

Katie admitted, "We're worried about Lily's mother. Something . . . happened to her when she came up here. She's not the same. So we've come up to check it out."

"So there are no movie stars."

Katie shook her head.

"And there are no cool clubs."

Katie shook her head.

"And there are no boutiques that only cater to the summer people, with a Dartmouth boy behind the cash register wearing chinos, with salt and sand in his hair, and crinkles around his eyes when he smiles, working there as a part-time job so he can meet a cool chick to go with him on an around-the-world cruise in his sail-boat, called the—"

"No," said Katie.

Madigan opened her purse and snapped it shut again. "So fill in the blank: In this town there is _____."

"A death beyond death, that seeks the life of the living."

"Um, yeah. Other than that. In this town there is _____."

"Diddly-squat."

Madigan nodded. "Diddly-squat," she repeated.

Katie confirmed, "Diddly-squat."

Madigan stuck her tongue up behind her upper lip so the lip bulged. She kept nodding, slowly.

She crossed her arms.

Very quietly, very neatly, she said to them, "Now get out of this room. Get out of this room and take your little bags with you and go away and do not come back to this room."

Lily snatched at her backpack and started to trundle out.

Katie protested, "You can't just—"

"Your little bag. And out. You go. Or death."

Madigan's skin, light and sweet as frosting, began to shiver.

Katie took her suitcase and ran for the door.

They shut it before the screaming started.

The main street of town was called Main Street. Some of the stores with big windows were normal stores, like a convenience store and a hardware store and a clothing store, but most of them were places where psychics told your fortune or spoke to the dead for you. The little psychic shops were called things like That's the Spirit! and Medium Rare.

"So, chums, where do we go first?" asked Jasper. He inspected the street up and down with crisp turns of the head.

Katie was looking uneasily up at the hotel window where Madigan could be seen gesturing with curled knuckles while indignantly yowping into her iSquawk. "You know," said Katie, "my Horror Hollow instincts suggest that maybe leaving someone alone in the town of the undead isn't a great idea. Kind of like running upstairs when you're being chased by a madman. Or finding a book of spells and reading the one labeled 'Unleash the King of Pestilence.'"

Lily said sympathetically, "That was a bad week for you."

Katie puffed out her breath and clapped her hands together. "My mom will kill me if something eats my cousin's brain. I mean, unless no one notices."

"Well," said Lily uneasily, "it's not even dark yet. We're not going to go far."

"I guess," Katie agreed. "I just hope Madigan doesn't do anything stupid."

As they walked away, Drgnan said, "Fleeing upstairs from evil is not always a mistake. It is said that Saint Klrkvm of Warwick fled a demon by running up a tower staircase. When he got to the top and ran out of steps, the demon began to laugh and reached out its long claw. But Saint Klrkvm kept running, and stairs unfolded themselves in the crystal air, as he ran up toward the clouds, toward the stars, toward the dome of heaven. . . ."

"Wow," said Lily admiringly. She thought he told a story really well.

Drgnan mused for a moment and said softly, "You know, are we not all like Saint Klrkvm, for do we not—" The moral to Drgnan's story was cut off as they went into a store. The glass door swung shut.

They left behind them the one lit window in

the battered old hotel. One solitary light behind an iron balcony railing.

The four friends were in a clothing store. There were the usual clothes—sweaters, shirts, socks, and a big display of gloves and mittens for the winter—but also they noticed winding-sheets, in which ghosts wrap themselves, and, for the vampire clients, tuxedos with tailcoats and white bow ties.

Katie and Lily walked through racks of skirts toward the cash register. Katie said, "I wish we weren't always like tense and crazy when we went places. It would be nice to just go someplace for fun."

Lily nodded sadly.

Katie tried to perk her up by saying gently, "Hey, won't it be cool when we're older? And when we have our own cars? I mean, cars that don't have to be driven by a robot? Won't it be amazing when I can just come by your house and pick you up? And we won't have to ask our parents. And then all of us can go and stay someplace for the weekend, and see whatever we want, and go shopping wherever we want, and eat whatever we want?"

"I hope," muttered Jasper, "we do not ever shop again at a place where vampires can buy *clip-on bow ties.* You would think with all of eternity in front of them, they could take the time to learn a simple knot."

Lily did love the idea of them older—if they ever did get older—all of them in their twenties, maybe, or even in college—going to stay at the Outer Banks in North Carolina, or the Rocky Mountains, and having fun. But she didn't want to think about what it would be like when she was too old to ask her parents about things. She wanted her parents just the way they were. Or, she thought somberly, just the way they *had been.*

Katie asked the cashier about Lily's mother—whether a woman had come into the store a few days before, a woman who wasn't from town.

The cashier hadn't noticed anyone specially.

The four friends wandered up the street. There was a little gift shop. A witch wind chime tinkled when they went in. They passed in a line along the racks and glass counters, looking at the little wooden houses, the jewelry, the hand-dipped candles, the chunks of amethyst, and some pudgy calico zombie dolls stuffed with sweet-scented potpourri. ("Rose from the crypt? Don't delay! With these fine dolls, no smell of decay!")

Lily and Katie went up to the cash register while Jasper and Drgnan investigated some juggling batons.

"I'm locking up soon," said the lady behind the counter. She was an older lady in a flowy sort of dress and running shoes, wearing blue feather earrings in her ears. She was turned to the side, with one eye staring straight out the front window, watching the street. "It's going to be dark out." She looked at the kids. "We own the town during the day. They own it at night."

Lily was often a little shy, so Katie stepped forward and explained that they were wondering if a woman had come in a few days before, a woman from out of town.

"You mean the woman with the car that rolled down the hill?" The lady nodded. "Yeah. Yeah, she came in. She was walking around town, seeing the sights, and she came in."

"She did?" said Lily excitedly.

"How did she act?" Katie asked. "Weird?"

The lady behind the counter sighed. "Hard to tell, in this town." She flipped open a logbook beside the cash register. "I thought she acted weird. I mean, she came in here the morning after her car was totaled, and she was completely cheerful."

Lily and Katie exchanged a look. Did this mean that Lily's mother had already been replaced by the undead?

"She kept talking about her daughter and how wonderful she was. She bought . . ." (The lady ran her finger down a column of notes.)

"She bought a turquoise necklace for her daughter as a present. She said it was time for her daughter to have some jewelry." The woman walked over to one of the glass cases. "It looked like this one. Made by a local craftsman." She pointed at a necklace with a big blue stone surrounded by arms of silver. Lily and Katie went and looked at it. The necklace glittered in the display lights. The woman explained, "It forms a kind of a stylized ankh, the Egyptian symbol of eternal life." She shrugged. "The woman said she wanted it for her daughter. She wanted to protect her. You must be the daughter."

Lily's eyes were filled with tears. Her mother had bought a necklace for her. Her first necklace. The ankh. The symbol of eternal life. Because her mother wanted her to always be safe.

She couldn't answer the lady that yes, she was the daughter. She had too big a lump in her throat.

Katie put her arm around her friend.

The saleslady saw what was wrong, and nodded sadly and solemnly.

"Got her, did they?" she asked gently.

Katie frowned at the woman and drew Lily away.

As they left the store, the woman called after them, "Get off the streets by dark! It becomes their town!"

The door tinkled as it swung shut.

It was almost five o'clock.

"This is awful," said Lily. "I hate the thought of all these unquiet spirits. I want all these people to be happy."

Drgnan smiled at her. "It would be good if they could move on," he said. "They should follow the path to the light that lies beyond the farthest sphere of fire."

"Or have a stupendous picnic," suggested Jasper, "with rides." His eyes sparkled at the thought of zombies on the Tilt-A-Whirl, slamming side to side.

"Things are going to be closing soon," said Katie. "It's almost five o'clock."

Lily suggested, "Could we ask in the convenience store? Maybe she went in for some food."

"Good idea," said Katie.

"Swell," said Jasper.

But Drgnan just stared and looked tense. "You go on to the convenience store," he said. "I am going to go back to the hotel to check on your cousin Madigan."

"Huh? Why?" Katie asked.

"Because when we went into the gift shop, her light was on and the window was closed." He pointed.

The French window onto the balcony was open. The curtains hung disheveled. And the room inside was dark.

13

If you're in a town of the undead, you need to be the life of the party.

That, at least, is what Madigan Westlake-Duvet thought to herself as she pulled on her clubbing clothes. Of course, she didn't believe that Todburg was a town of the undead. She didn't believe in the undead in the first place. She just thought her cousin was kookoo. So she thought that somewhere out there in the festering night, there was a dance club just waiting to see some New York chic, some Upper East Side moves.

Madigan pulled on a pair of black Mon Trésor night-pants and a sparkly, sequined cami-blouse by Brunt of New York. How could she not make a splash in those great pants and her cool sling-back pumps?

Like a splash in a lake of embalming fluid.

She sat at the mirror, carefully applying her makeup. While she defined her eyes, she thought vaguely about how amazing she looked. She was going to be like one of those tornadoes that hits upstate New York towns and rips the whole place apart. *Isn't it tornadoes? Or maybe it's some other kind of plague they have here,* she thought to herself. *Like sores or frogs or wild dogs or something.*

There was a click behind her. She sat up straight. It was kind of a creepy hotel, and she didn't love hearing weird clicks behind her.

In the mirror, she looked back over her shoulder.

Behind her, the window that led out onto the balcony swung open. No one was there.

Telling herself not to be afraid, she kept on defining her eyes. But now she kept an eye, too, on the dark place behind her in the mirror.

There was nothing there.

In the mirror.

Because vampires don't show up in mirrors.

So she could not see the boy who was sneaking across the room toward her, his webbed hand outstretched for her neck.

If she had turned around, she would have seen him.

Instead she continued to define her eyes, staring at herself.

He opened his mouth wide. His fangs glinted in the lamplight. Softly, he panted.

Madigan swiveled to grab her black vinyl Dave Brollo clutch with the blue piping.

She looked up and saw a boy standing a few feet away, his jaw hanging open, preparing to jump at her neck.

"Sorry," said Madigan. "I didn't realize I was in the mouth-breather waiting room. Why don't I just take myself somewhere else?" She grabbed the room keys off the dresser, spun them once around her finger on their ring, and popped them into her clutch.

Madigan thought the boy seemed weird. He kept staring at her. Staring as if possessed.

Oh. Wait. *Not weird at all.* That was how most boys reacted to her.

"Who *are* you?" she demanded.

He didn't say a word.

"Did you just climb in through the balcony window?" she asked.

Bashfully, the vampire boy nodded.

"You climbed up to the balcony just to get in here and see me?"

The vampire boy shrugged. He locked his thumbs together and flapped his hands, miming bat-flight.

"That's great, Marcel Marceau. Your soul soars like an eagle. What I'm asking is, did you climb up here just to see me? Because that's actually kind of romantic."

He sized her up, wondering if he could hold down her arms for long enough to drain her blood. She sized him up, wondering whether he would look at all okay if she gave him a makeover to add a little Uptown Manhattan to that cow-pasture fashion. She walked in a circle around him, inspecting his duds.

"Replace the hoodie," she mused, "with a button-down oxford. And those awful over-sized jeans with a pair of Polo by Ralph Lauren slacks in Nantucket red . . . And those grubby sneakers have got to go. Maybe some calfskin penny loafers from Plunder House of London . . . Yeah . . ." She laughed. "It would be a great story to tell the girls back home. A country boy who loved me so much he climbed a balcony to get to me. Then I *remade* him, I'll tell them. Like Dr. Franken-stein. 'It's aliiiive! It's aliiiive!'"

The thunder outside crashed.

Madigan stared at him and tapped her cheek thoughtfully. "All right, prowler-puss. Are you boyfriend material?" She raised her eyebrow.

The vampire boy had never considered whether he was boyfriend material. He was a little confused, but getting kind of enraged, because really he just wanted to drink someone's blood, and all these insane people kept bashing him in the nose, siccing tarantulas on him, and telling him his sneakers were gross.

Madigan asked, "How are you . . . at *necking*?" She batted her eyelashes.

That was all he needed. He jumped.

The lamp crashed to the floor. The room went dark.

Keep Your Nose in the Air at ...

SNOTT ACADEMY

There's no time at Snott for history or biology—not with all the passion and all the fashion! Madigan Westlake-Duvet is a queen bee with a mean sting. Come hang out with her and her clique—the coolest and cruelest in the school!*

You know you want to. You better start buying these books *now*, and I mean *NOW now*:

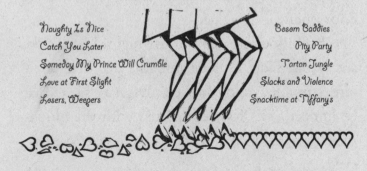

Naughty Is Nice

Catch You Later

Someday My Prince Will Crumble

Love at First Slight

Losers, Weepers

Bosom Baddies

Pity Party

Tartan Jungle

Slacks and Violence

Snacktime at Tiffany's

---

*If you're good enough at being bad, and won't be a crybaby like you usually are, and won't wear that brown thing you wore last Thursday, what-*ever* that was.

14

Madigan screamed. She whapped the vampire with her clutch. She jumped up on one of the beds and bounced. He jumped up too. She bounced to the other bed. He bounced after her. She bounced back to the first one. He bounced too.

Back and forth, back and forth, back and forth through the shadows.

This was when Drgnan Pghlik kicked the door open.

"Back, foul creature of the night!" he yelled, and vaulted off a chair into the air. The vampire stumbled and ducked. Drgnan kicked as he jumped. His foot connected with the bloodsucker's head, and the vampire went briefly cross-eyed.

Recovering quickly, the vampire lurched toward his new opponent. He seized Drgnan by the shoulders and swooped his jaws toward the monk's neck.

Drgnan toppled backward! The beast was upon him!

Snap! The iron-strong jaws closed on air.

Snap! They closed again, closer to Drgnan's throat.

Snap! Once more, and Drgnan would have a hole the size of a fist in his jugular vein.

He could feel the vampire's clammy breath on his skin. He fought, but the undead kid was strong—stronger than a normal human.

A drop of cold spit hung down from the fangs, cold as grave-dirt; it dropped like a spider, and splotched on Drgnan's cheek. He flinched.

And then the vampire lunged for the kill.

And gagged. Choked. Snarled in midair. Madigan Westlake-Duvet had grabbed him around the neck with her nautical-themed Hermès scarf, a silk neckerchief with a pattern of anchors and dolphins she had actually found ugly, even dowdy, when she had been given it as a door prize at a party for attractive French socialite Armand de Loublie-Doublée, newly arrived from Paris, where he was making a movie with—

Oh. Sorry.

The scarf held the vampire back from Drgnan's neck! Madigan had saved Drgnan's life. The vampire growled and swayed, suspended a few inches away from a satisfying chomp.

Enraged, he turned to seize the girl.

Drgnan grabbed the monster.

Then he yelped in pain—the vampire had sunk his teeth into the monk's arm. Drgnan kicked at the bloodthirsty teen, trying to dislodge him.

Madigan beat the vampire's head with her clutch.

The vampire didn't budge. He kept drinking Drgnan's blood, like Drgnan's arm was a Krazy Straw.

Drgnan dragged the boy sideways toward the bathroom door.

When they were there, he kicked as hard as he could. The vampire clung like a tick. Drgnan kicked again—and this time, Madigan kicked too.

The vampire gasped in pain and released the monk's arm. He fell backward into the bathroom.

Drgnan slammed the bathroom door shut. He leaned against it. It heaved as the vampire crashed against it, trying to get out. Drgnan grimaced, put his back against the door, and dug his heels into the wall-to-wall carpet.

Inside, the vampire prepared to push with all his strength. He braced himself and took a deep breath.

And then felt a tickle on his foot.

Let me stop for just a second of complicated and technical scientific discussion. I'm sorry about this, but it's important.

Now, remember that Lily, Katie, and the rest had recently been palling around with spies.* Spies had helped smuggle them across the border of Delaware. Spies had chased them up and down the mountains of that state. In many ways, they were practically spies themselves. And as I said earlier in this thrilling tale, it is an established scientific fact, long known to naturalists, that the bathroom in a spy's hotel suite is the favored habitat of . . . that's right . . . tarantulas.

There, at the vampire's foot, was the Adirondack tarantula he'd met a few days before.

So then the yelling, and the hitting, and the scrambling around started. The hissing of the spider, the hissing of the vampire. Two old enemies reunited. *Bang! Whap! Blam!*

"Shall we go rejoin the others?" asked Drgnan.

"Sure, baldy," said Madigan Westlake-Duvet, with a wink that suggested she was no longer so interested in a date with a vampire.

---

*In *Agent Q, or The Smell of Danger!*

15

There was an old theater or opera house on Midnight Boulevard, just off Main.

It was a run-down building that had been painted white a long time before. Now there were dark cracks in all the paint, and the shingles were splitting. Katie, Jasper, and Lily looked up at it.

There was a sign out front on an easel. It said:

TODBURG COMMUNITY THEATER

PRESENTS

AN EVENING
OF
DROLL ESCAPADES
AND
COMICAL SKITS

including
the "lady with a cold"
and another one
about a caveman.
Also, Mouso the Funny Magician.

HA! HA! HA!

$1.25

"Wow," said Katie. "That sounds completely lame."

Jasper said, "Why, I have to agree, Katie. A lady with a cold does not sound like good comedy. I don't believe in laughing at people with headaches."

Katie said, "The 'Ha! Ha! Ha!' actually makes it sound like the most unfunny thing in the universe."

"Let's go in," said Lily. "Maybe my mother came to see the show."

"Perhaps they serve popcorn," said Jasper. He was kind of a popcorn fiend.

They walked into the theater. In the lobby, there were stacks of old seats. On the walls hung posters from shows of yesteryear.

There was a light on in the ticket window. There was a little man there with a little mustache under his red nose. He had tired eyes, and what was left of his hair was tired too.

"Excuse me," said Lily. "We're looking for a woman from out of town who might have come into the theater a few days ago to see the show. We're wondering if you have any information about her. She has brown hair, and she was wearing—"

"It's a dollar and a quarter for a ticket."

"Oh," explained Lily, "we don't really want to see the show. If it's okay, I just wanted to ask you about my mother."

The man gripped the counter. "If you're not waiting for tickets, please get out of the line," he said. "There are other customers waiting."

"They're my friends," said Lily.

"We offer group discounts."

"We're not really interested in seeing the show."

"Then please step out of line, thank you," said the man.

Katie came forward. "We're looking for her mother. Could you answer a few questions?"

The man looked at her with his sad schnauzer eyes. "You might be the only people coming to the show tonight," he said. "Three tickets would be three seventy-five. I can give you a group discount of seventy-five cents. That would bring it down to three dollars on the button."

His voice was a sad little voice that might belong to a weepy dog in a cartoon, a dog who couldn't be bothered to chase a crazy comic squirrel with schemes.

"You will enjoy the droll escapades and comical skits," the ticket seller said. "You will find the comedians will really tickle your funny bone."

The kids looked at one another. Then they each got out a dollar and gave the man the money.

He punched a button three times, and three tickets curled out in a strip. He handed them to the kids.

Then he walked out of the office into the lobby.

"Okay," he said in his depressing little voice. "Now let's go into the theater." He pushed the doors open and they walked in.

It was an old and pretty barren theater. There were rows of folding chairs. There was a stage. Many of the lightbulbs were out.

The man said, "Who does all of the acts? Horace G. Tubley does." His voice echoed in the big, empty room. The man said, "Who is Horace G. Tubley?" He put his hand on his own chest. "I am Horace G. Tubley." He sounded as if he were apologizing for it. He sounded miserable to be Horace G. Tubley.

He shuffled forward down the aisle. "I have lots of comic characters. For one, I am a caveman. I have a cave made out of cardboard. I go into the cave and I come out of the cave. And then there is all kinds of business. That one is very funny and droll. In another, I dress up in a wig, then I make believe I am an old woman with a cold. I speak in a comical voice that entertains the audience. In another number, called 'Little Betty's Prank,' I'm a girl. I have a pigtail wig, and I dress in a polka-dot frock. If you yell, 'Betty, what's the prank?' then I make something up. Then you yell, 'Really, Betty, do tell us the prank, Betty.' And . . ." He trailed off unhappily.

Lily and Katie were looking at him with eyes full of pity. It was astounding: He was perhaps the least funny person they had ever met. Lily wanted to bring him a busload of kids to watch his show, but then she thought they might make fun of him for being so dull. Katie just was thinking she wanted to buy him an ice-cream cone and tell him to feel better, but in fact he was so dull that most of the time he was talking she had thought about this ice-cream cone and what flavor it should be, instead of listening to him, and she hadn't heard a word about his comic acts.

"The woman sat over there," he said. He pointed at a chair.

The kids stared.

"The woman who came the other night," explained Horace G. Tubley. "She sat in 3-H."

Lily made her way along the rows. She came to the chair and looked down at it. She reached out and touched the wooden seat. Her mother had sat there hours before she had been replaced.

"I asked her what act she wanted me to do. In the end, I did a bear act, where I am a bear. I do it mainly with my left half. Then I did Mouso the Funny Magician. I am also Mouso, that magician. I don't do any real magic, but the theater is haunted, and the ghost helps me do tricks. I can't do the tricks anymore, though, because the ghost has disappeared now. So instead, if you asked me, I would recommend you ask me to do either 'Betty's Prank,' or 'Time for the Bears!'"

He kept talking, but Lily was not listening. She was leaning down.

There was a little paper bag under seat 3-H. It was carefully folded over.

She picked it up. Maybe her mother had dropped it.

Lily opened up the bag.

Inside lay a turquoise necklace with its price tag still attached.

16

Lily held up the turquoise necklace. "Katie! Jasper!" she called. "It's the necklace my mom bought me!"

They walked sideways through the rows of chairs to stand by her.

"If the theater were still haunted, if the ghost were still here," Horace G. Tubley said, "then Mouso the Funny Magician would have been able to tell you what was inside the paper bag. The ghost would have checked. Then she would have told me. Then I would have said, 'I wonder what is inside the paper bag.' Then I would have made a pun on the word 'necklace.'" He thought hard. He clearly could not think of a good pun. He mumbled other "necklace" words, like "pendant" and "choker," then shook his head despairingly.

Katie lifted the necklace off Lily's fingers and let it dangle. "It's really nice, Lily," she said.

Jasper, however, looked thoughtful. He turned back to Horace G. Tubley and called to him, "Mr. Tubley, sir . . . Tell us about this ghost who used to haunt the old place—who used to assist you with your magic."

"She was an actress named Vivian de NeVoshka. Actual name, Mabel Glutt. She said she was from French-occupied Russia, or Russian-occupied France, but really she was from Wanskuck, Rhode Island. She was an actress at the theater seventy or eighty years ago. She kept on extending her farewell appearances until finally she died, and even then she did not want to take a final bow. So she kept on walking across the stage as a ghost, and she played hilarious and droll pranks with the theater lights and suchlike. Finally she frightened everyone away so no one came to see plays anymore except dead people. Now every night, dead people come, but never any live people anymore. I worked her into my act of Mouso the Funny Magician. We would do tricks. For example, I would put a thing on a table, and if it was a girl's barrette, for example, I would say, 'Ladies and gentleman, now it is *hair*, and now it is gone!' or some similar joke. And then the ghost would take the barrette away. And it would be like magic—funny magic."

Katie was going to jump out a window if the man kept talking, his voice was so sad and boring.

Jasper said, "But she is gone now?"

Horace G. Tubley nodded. "She just up and disappeared. Now the theater is not haunted, but still, all the dead keep on coming every night to see the show and you know, the show must go on. In fact, the dead will be arriving soon. They never pay a dollar and twenty-five cents to see the show, which is what I charge for the show, a dollar and twenty-five cents. And if I—"

"You know, Mr. Tubley," said Jasper, "I would be awfully interested to know when this ghost vanished."

There was a sound in the lobby. The doors to the theater slammed open.

Horace G. Tubley just had time to say, "She vanished a couple of days ago," before there was a hideous howling.

The dead had arrived for their evening matinee.

17

The dead came shambling in a horde. They stank like decay. The stench was sweet—sickly sweet—which somehow was worse than just being moldy. They filled the aisles. They did not seem to see one another. In their eyes was a look of hunger and desperation. The vampires' chins glistened with drool. Their footfalls were heavy on the carpet. They did not remember how to carry their own weight well. Ghosts wafted above them.

The gruesome tide filled the room.

Katie, Lily, and Jasper backed toward the stage. The dead groaned and pointed.

"What are we going to do?" Katie gasped.

"Sit tight, chums," said Jasper. "If worse

comes to worst, we do have the prototype of the Astounding High-Pressure Holy Water Extruder Gun." He cradled it in his arms and looked sharp.

"Don't make them mad," said Lily. "They don't have any reason to kill us. They just want a show."

"Or to take control of your mind," said Horace G. Tubley, who was now standing right next to them. "The ghosts can take over your mind, if they touch you too long. They like to do that. Then they can have a body again." He looked down at his own body. "None of them have tried to take over my body," he said, sounding a little disappointed. "I have a fungus on my feet. I have to wear ziplock baggies as socks."

The dead did not stop at their assigned seats, if they had ever been issued assigned seats. They kept on moving forward toward the living. They surrounded the three kids. A roomful of pale, purpling, rotting faces. Swirls of ghost-smoke. Scratchy bat wings. Wide, awful eyes. All clustered around Lily, Katie, and Jasper. Staring. Peering.

Katie clambered backward up onto the stage and dragged Lily up behind her. Jasper leaped up and landed in a crouch, the squirt gun at the ready.

The moaning and rasping of the dead was overpowering now, as was their stench.

"Let's run for the back door," said Jasper.

"I would not run," said Horace G. Tubley, crossing his arms. "They would not like it if you tried to get away. That would not be comical nor droll, unless while you were running, you were to slip upon a peel or rind. The dead people would be very angry."

Jasper asked (somewhat testily), "So what do you suggest?"

Horace looked at the crowd. "You had better," he said, "put on a show."

* * *

"So," said Madigan Westlake-Duvet. "Your dress. Made by?"

Drgnan Pghlik explained, "It is not a dress. It is called a 'habit.'"

"And it's made by?"

"Seven old men singing hymns through the night."

Madigan thought about this. "Toothless?"

"They have eight or nine teeth, between them."

"So when you say *old men*, you don't mean old Italian designers with manes of white hair and ultrawide lapels."

"We must be quiet and watchful, if we are to find our friends."

"Yeah," said Madigan, "I can find my friends by walking into Nocturne on Fifth Avenue and taking a table near the ice sculptures. Those aren't the losers we're looking for."

Drgnan Pghlik frowned. Night had fallen. Despite the streetlamps, the town was dark and murky. Occasionally, in the alleys, something would slowly creep.

The two kids, monk and fashionista, moved carefully down the sidewalk. Drgnan Pghlik was ready to spring into action if the undead made their move.

Madigan hissed, "Hey. Baldy."

He looked back toward her.

She asked, "So was the dress ready-to-wear?"

Drgnan scowled.

She said, "I mean, your 'habit.' Was it off the rack?"

The monk turned and kept on walking, hands out in front of him and ready for action.

She plucked at his hood to make sure it hung straight on his back, and in a high voice, sang out, "I think I smell something tailor-made!" The way she sang "made," it went *may-yade!* Then she sang, "I can tell the friendlings he wears hand *woven*!"

Singing on a street haunted by the dazed

dead is not a good idea. It really tends to stir up the crowd and attract notice.

No sooner had Drgnan turned to frown at the New York girl than a tall, tall vampire in striped pants stepped out of an alley and began following them at a distance.

"Down here," said Drgnan, guiding her down a side street.

"Mm," said Madigan. "I like how you grab my arm. Hurry me along."

They were passing a hulking building that gleamed a dull gray in the distant streetlights.

It was a theater.

From out of the theater came an awful sound. It was like someone was shouting, loudly, earnestly, but on musical notes (kind of).

"Jasper's in trouble," said Drgnan. "Big trouble."

"Huh?"

"Because otherwise," Drgnan explained, "he would not be attempting to sing."

"What do you mean?"

The monk was too busy examining the theater to answer. "Down here," he said. "It looks like there's a back door."

There was a door with an old panel of wood over the window, painted with a faded star. Drgnan tugged and pushed at the release bar. He explained to Madigan, "Jasper has the kind of voice that's only good for singing the National Anthem. And even then, to his sorrow, he cannot hit the high notes."

With a smack and a creak, the door swung open.

They could see into the backstage of the theater. Curtains. Rope. Levers. A horse on wheels. And shadows.

They went in, silently. Madigan carefully closed the door behind them.

They were behind the backdrop, off to the side. Jasper, indeed, was on the stage, belting out a song. He was making up the words while Katie pounded out "Heart and Soul" on an upright piano.

"OU—TER—SPACE!
I like to fly up in
OU—TER—SPACE!
Zoom! Zoom!
Oh! How I like to
Fly, bumpa doo, pa doo pa doo pa doo."

I don't think I need to say his arms were spread wide.

Usually, when people sing something as stupid as "pa doo pa doo pa doo," they at least try to actually hit notes, which makes the words sound a little less awful. But hitting notes was not part of Jasper's skill set. He belted out the song in a kind of desperate, loud, robotic monotone.

And the zombies thought they'd never seen anything so magnificent in their lives. By which I mean deaths.

Drgnan sized up the situation. "Let us consider what action to take," he said, frowning. "The falcon circles above his prey before he swoops."

"No," said Madigan, as Lily Gefelty, dressed like a Victorian schoolmarm, clonked out onstage in giant shoes and began a song that started, "Oh Mr. Spaceman! You're out of this world!"

Madigan said, "No, no, no."

She walked toward the stage lights.

"Madigan," called Drgnan in a whisper. "What are you doing?"

She turned on her heel, walked back to him, put her finger delicately on his chin, and said, "Leave this one to me, baldy."

She blew him a kiss. Then she stormed out right onstage.

The lights were bright.

Katie stopped hammering on the piano.

"NO! NO! NO!" said Madigan. Her voice echoed through the theater. Everything stopped. Everyone stared at her.

The zombies and vampires and ghosts and ghouls stirred. Now here was a real beauty. Maybe time for a dance number. Things were picking up.

Madigan turned to Katie and rapped out, "You have lied to me! You have kidnapped me and brought me to this stupid town! You have left me alone so I was attacked by a blood-sucking sophomore! You have put my life in danger. But *I DRAW THE LINE AT SHOW TUNES!*" Her declaration rang and rang in the stunned auditorium. She screamed, "AND, CURTAIN!"

Nothing happened.

The crowd began to groan and growl.

She put her hand over her eyes so she could see them. She glared out at the sea of undead, the putrefying faces, the skeleton foreheads, the

sores. "Oh, shut up," she said. "Don't you dare boo me." (Lily thought that was not smart, considering it was an audience of ghosts.) "Hello! Shut up! I'm not scared. Look at you! Look at all of you! You're pathetic and old and dead! I am *never* going to be like you! I look out there and I see a bunch of washed-up people who don't even have a *heartbeat* anymore. Oh my gosh, I can't help but laugh at you all." She turned and looked at Drgnan. He was horrified. She winked at him. She turned back toward the undead audience, who were staggering forward, mooing and pawing at the air. She yelled out at them, "You think you're so totes scary. What's scarier than me, losers? What's scarier than *glamour*? And glitter? And—ta da—my fantabulosity!"

"Madigan," said Lily, gesturing wildly. "Madigan, this really isn't a good time for—"

The dead were roaring.

"I WILL NEVER BE LONELY, LOSERS!" Madigan exclaimed. "I LOOK OUT THERE, AND I SEE *FAILURE!* AND, PEEPS, *FAILURE* IS WHAT I HATE MOST OF—"

Katie tried to play the piano loudly over her. Lily rushed to Madigan's side and tried to push her offstage, which was a brave thing for Lily to try to do, since touching Madigan Westlake-Duvet was like punching a live fuse box.

The undead poured forward. They were screaming too now, though often there were no words. They crashed onto the stage.

Lily and Jasper dragged Madigan off left.

Katie scampered away from the piano.

Drgnan prepared to defend their flank.

And the dead, the evil dead, now angry, bitter, wishing to crush, rushed forward.

18

Confronted by a mob of yowling zombies, ghouls, and ghosts crashing forward over folding chairs, swiping their claws through the air, even Madigan Westlake-Duvet, debutante beauty of Snott Academy, realized that perhaps her audience was no longer as fascinated by her golden-haired, leggy, it-girl beauty as they had been a few minutes before. She turned to run.

The monster swarm catapulted up onto the stage.

Drgnan was already through the rear exit, holding the door open, shouting, "This way!"

Katie and Lily were hauling Madigan toward the door while Jasper, swinging the squirt gun around, guarded their retreat. Madigan squealed as she was flanked by ghouls.

Jasper pulled the trigger.

Holy water arced across the brutal crowd.

They screamed with displeasure. It stung.

Not enough to stop them—but definitely enough to surprise them.

Drgnan and the three girls ran out the door and into the cold November night.

"Up the street!" Lily cried. "To the Robo-Sedan!"

Jasper remained behind in the theater, firing into the crowd, hoping to gain his friends a little time. Ghosts curled away like smoke from the drizzle of liquid pain. Zombies growled and thudded forward, too dumb to flinch. Ghouls held their Playbills in front of their faces and swatted at the air, hoping by sheer luck to slash Dash.

Jasper realized he had to give up his rear-guard position and make a run for it. He hoped the others had gotten a chance to make it back to Main Street. He bolted out the door and slammed it behind him. He looked around quickly. Nothing there to block the door. So he left it and ran after his friends.

Monsters were coming out of the main theater doors, their dead throats groaning.

They blocked his way.

He started to spray them.

They backed up, howled, closed their eyes.

He sprinted past them, still spraying.

The blessed water shot in burning arcs through the air, splattering on decaying flesh, making it smoke.

And then, suddenly, he was out of water. The trigger clicked.

No more squirt gun.

He kept on running.

Meanwhile, Lily, Drgnan, and Madigan skittered around the corner onto Main Street. They had to find the car—and quickly!

Lily huffed and puffed past stores made

of wood and brick. She heard Madigan clacking along behind her, her sling-back La Nocha pumps slapping on the pavement.

Katie lingered behind, calling down Midnight Boulevard, "Come on, Jas! To the Robo-Sedan!" She saw the Boy Technonaut pelting toward her, far down the street, pursued by a cloud of specters and bats.

Jasper, fleeing from the horde of undead, knew that if they grabbed him, it would be a free-for-all. Ghosts would try to take over his mind, and zombies would try to devour his body. There were hundreds of them. He would be pulled limb from limb.

He reflected with disappointment that in a crowd like that, there would be lots of grabbing, and no one would really get their fair share. Believing so strongly in the ideals of justice and equality, he was horrified that he might be divided unevenly, with the slower zombies losing out to the faster, more grabby zombies.

It's not simply that life is unfair, thought

Jasper. *It appears that death is unfair too. And I call that rotten.*

So, he added to himself, with a lift of the eyebrow, *I shall just have to make sure that no zombies, slow or fast, feast on me tonight.* And he turned the corner onto Main Street.

A blinding light shone on Lily. She shielded her eyes from the beams. What was it? She blew her bangs up out of her eyes. She was terrified. . . .

Beside her Madigan reeled.

There was the sound of a car engine.

Suddenly Lily shouted with joy. The blinding lights were headlights. The Robo-Sedan had seen them and had started up! It was rolling toward them. Drgnan, Madigan, Lily, and Katie gathered around it. They grabbed the handles and pulled.

Nothing happened. It was locked.

"Um, hello?" Lily said. "We're with Jasper."

The robot sat in the driver's seat, obediently waiting for its master.

"My metal brother," said Drgnan through the window glass, "you must open your heart to us. Or at least your passenger-side doors."

The robot's glassy eyes faced forward. It showed no sign of having heard the children.

Bats began to spin in circles over their heads. Bats began to swoop down. They circled lower and lower.

And the robot chauffeur waited for orders from Jasper Dash.

Jasper charged toward the car. He could distantly see it, and his friends clustered around it. "GET IN! GET IN, CHUMS!" he screamed. But for some reason, his friends didn't budge, but just stood there, looking right at him.

And then, drifting down over the rooftops like autumn fog, came tendrils of ghost. Softly wafting, spinning on currents, the ghosts dribbled down along the street. In the eddies of smoke were bits of phantom face or finger: a watchful eye, a mouth that kissed, a delicate hand. They were coming together, getting more solid.

Jasper passed through the first several ghost-clouds, forcing the spirits to disperse.

But then he felt the coldness in them. They were trying to touch him long enough to take him over. Streamers of fog hung over him. He panted as he ran, and ghost poured into his parched, open mouth.

Now, usually, ghosts can't do anything to people. They just blow around and go, "Whoo, whoo." They stare out over castle battlements, looking sappy. But the ghosts of Todburg were not your usual ghosts. For years, they had been living in a town of incredible haunting power—a place where this world meets the next world. So if they grabbed onto someone and held on to them for a while—a minute or so—then they could actually take that person over. They could control that person. Unless that person was Horace G. Tubley, in which case their horror at his bad puns, his poor comic timing, and his rampant foot fungus frightened them away.

But Jasper Dash—now he was another story entirely. He was a true prize for a ghost.

The spirits clustered around him and grabbed with their soft, foggy paws. If they could take him over, if they could seize upon his brain, they would have youth again, and strength, and agility—all the benefits of his adventurous lifestyle.* As he ran, they rubbed up against his face. They dove into his open throat.

He staggered. They slipped into his nostrils and over his tongue.

He coughed—gagged. Death was in him. He paused for a minute, hand on a storefront. He tried to catch his breath. He couldn't. The ghosts roiled around inside of him. He could tell his thinking was getting cloudy.

A Victorian porch . . . Granny on the rocker . . . There's old Silas, coming up the

---

*And his brimming, daily glass of Gargletine Brand Breakfast Drink™. It's pep in a tumbler! So kids, don't forget to gulp your glass *today!*

bridle-path. . . . Creak, creak . . . A long, fine summer afternoon this was. Why, he could stay like this forever, sitting on this porch, reading, while—

Jasper forced himself awake. Other people's memories were flooding his brain. They were fighting to take control.

Jasper staggered. He was losing the fight.

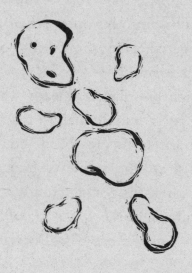

19

Lily saw Jasper collapse onto his knees. She looked up at the circling bats. She looked down the street. Shadowy, smudged figures were appearing in a ring around the fallen Boy Technonaut.

Then Lily saw Jasper reach up and, with the butt of the water gun, smash a plate-glass window.

Glass cascaded down. Jasper staggered away to avoid getting cut, but still, some fragments hit him, and they stung.

The pain woke him out of his dream of summer days in 1842 and railroad work in 1850. He jumped through the broken window.

Far away, Lily called his name.

But he knew if he ran straight toward his friends, toward the Robo-Sedan, he'd never make it.

So he had smashed the window to a flower shop called Pushing Up the Daisies.

He ran to the back room. The ghosts drifted in through the broken window and began to solidify again. They were tall and gaunt and they trailed wisps of white. Their faces were young, but were weird and torn. Smoke drifted from their eyes. They floated through the shop, waiting to grab their victim again. He would never get away.

They came upon him at the back of the store.

By the sink.

He was filling up his water gun.

He saw the specters and popped the gun's water tank shut.

He flipped a switch. The blue light went on, which meant the water was being quickly blessed.

The ghosts touched him. They stroked his

face. They whispered words he could only half hear, calling him "Daddy" and "Mommy" and "Charlie."

The light on his gun turned green, and he pulled the trigger.

Water shot out of the gun, scattering the spooks.

Jasper made a dash for the broken window.

Now he was back on the street, and his way was clear. He waved his hands at the car, which was blocks away. The engine revved.

"UNLOCK!" he yelled.

The doors unlocked.

Drgnan, Lily, Madigan, and Katie scrambled in.

"Oh, look," said Madigan, as she slammed the door. "Somehow I ended up on Drgnan's lap."

The car accelerated toward Jasper.

Now the zombies were coming out of side alleys. The vampire-bats had settled to the ground and were becoming full-fledged vampires again. The ghouls were hopping along, squawking in their weird language.

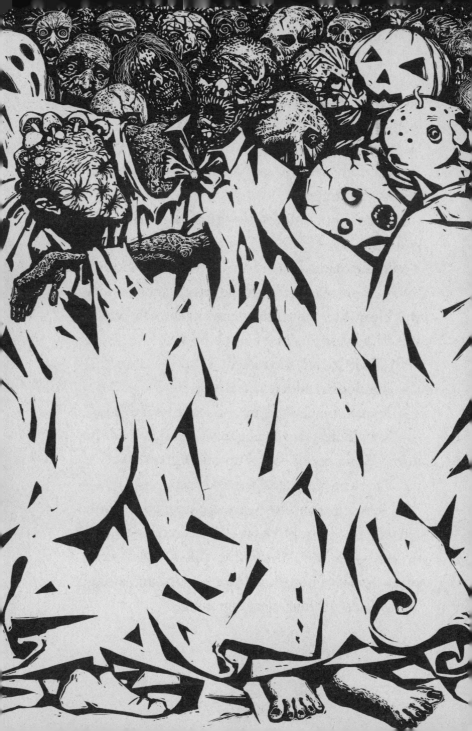

Jasper was seized by monsters. Claws were all over his shirt. Fangs surrounded his face like a shark-tooth necklace. And on his leg—poised to bite—was a deadly poisonous and very irritable Adirondack tarantula.

The Boy Technonaut struggled. He heard a high screech—booming—getting louder! His head swiveled wildly!

It was brakes. It was motion.

The Robo-Sedan slammed into zombies. Undead went flying.

Jasper was half-freed. He kicked out with his foot. Missed.

But the tarantula, hungry and bugged, flew off his leg—through the air—and landed on the face of a vampire.

The vampire was hissing, the tarantula was growling, Jasper was punching, and the door to the Robo-Sedan swung open, whacking a fiend in the belly.

Lily reached out, grabbed Jasper, and yanked.

The robot floored it.

Jasper struggled to pull his legs fully into the car. He yelled and kicked as the monsters dropped away behind them.

The Boy Technonaut flung himself onto Lily's feet. She slammed the door.

The car sped up . . . shot into third gear, fourth . . .

There was a line of zombies standing in its way.

The car swerved, slalom, around them.

"Ha ha!" Jasper cried.

But the robot made a bleating noise—a 1960s hearse with flames painted around the tires was backing out of a garage, right in their way. They narrowly avoided it.

The hearse gave chase. Two vampires drove it.

The Robo-Sedan screeched around a corner.

"Oh, look," said Madigan. "Centripetal force just threw my arm right around Drgnan."

She stared meanly at Lily.

Miserably, Lily mumbled, "I think you mean centrifugal."

Jasper rolled down the window with a crank. He leaned out and pointed the gun backward. Like an old gangster movie, he peppered the oncoming vehicle with holy water.

We could have a long car chase here. The bridge is still out, for example, so someone might have to jump the chasm to make it out of town.

But why? We already know the car can fly.

"REV UP THE JETS!" Jasper ordered.

And with a burst that threw everyone backward in their seats ("Oh, look," said Madigan, "the force of sudden acceleration threw my face right against Drgnan's shoulder."), the Robo-Sedan roared off the road, up into the sky.

It hurtled away from the cursed town. Against a backdrop of scratchy dead trees, it propelled itself cloudward.

And then they were floating, witchlike, before the moon.

Todburg lay behind them, tiny, on the ground.

20

The Robo-Sedan soared through the night.

The kids had managed to catch their breath after their terrifying retreat.

"We should not think of this as a retreat," Jasper said. "We did accomplish one thing by going to Todburg."

"Yeah," said Madigan. "We lost a suitcase full of Fifth Avenue's most fashion-forward winter collections."

(Her suitcases were still sitting in the hotel room. At that very moment, zombies were timidly unfolding her Oscar de la Renta suits and holding them up to the light.)

"No," said Jasper. "What we have accomplished, chums, is this: I believe we know what has happened to Lily's mother."

Everyone turned to him. Drgnan said, "How is that?"

"Lily," said Jasper, "are you thinking what I'm thinking?"

Lily nodded solemnly. She said, "That really is her body back at my house. But she's been taken over."

"By the ghost from the theater," said Jasper.

"The actress," said Lily. "Vivian de NeVoshka."

"Actual name, Mabel Glutt."

"From Wanskuck, Rhode Island."

"Oh . . . ," said Katie. She put her hand on her forehead. "Wow. Wow. I did not think of that at all."

Lily said, "I bet that's why the necklace was dropped on the floor. My mother was still herself the second day in Todburg. She went to the gift shop and she—she bought me that necklace. Then she went to see the comedy show at the theater. While Horace

G. Tubley was doing his Mouso the Funny Magician act—"

"With the help," Jasper said, "of undead assistant Vivian de NeVoshka—"

"—the ghost saw her chance to occupy the body of a living woman. So it . . ." Lily was getting visibly upset. "It must have appeared near my mom and held on to her for long enough to take over her mind. Maybe Mom struggled or . . . or something . . . and dropped the necklace in its bag. Or maybe she didn't struggle at all. Maybe she just forgot about the bag when the ghost took her over."

"And forgot about you," said Madigan, cracking her gum.

Katie said, "And forgot what you looked like. She just knew vaguely that she had a husband, and a daughter named Lily."

"She could have found our home address on her driver's license," said Lily. "She used a credit card from my mom's wallet to hire a rental car, and she drove back to Pelt."

Katie said, "So the woman in your house now really is your mother—but at the same time, really isn't?"

"Exactly," said Lily.

The Robo-Sedan rocked with air turbulence as it shot through layers of cloud.

"Oh, look," said Madigan. "I have to put my other arm around Drgnan Pghlik to steady myself because of air turbulence."

Katie looked aggravated. She looked out the window, while inside herself, she threw a miniature tantrum, slamming her imaginary hands and feet on the floor of her brain-house.

With a long, mean look at Lily and Katie, Madigan said to Drgnan, "Aren't we getting cozy?"

Drgnan suggested, "You might sit beside me instead of on me. My legs are falling asleep."

"Okay," said Madigan, "is that one of your monklike secret sayings, in which you mean that you don't know how to go forward in our flirtship, or is it—"

"There is no blood going to my legs. They are falling asleep."

"I hear you're quite a dancer," said Madigan, shifting to the side. She had heard from Katie that Katie had taken Drgnan to her school dance a few weeks before.

Drgnan said uncomfortably, "I dance to celebrate the spinning and turning of all things in the universal vortex."

"You know," said Madigan, walking her fingers up Drgnan's monastic cowl, "you could come down to New York and go to Snott Academy's big dance with me."

At this, Katie was furious. She turned toward them. "WHAT?!?" she shouted.

"It's not like Drgnan's going *out* with you," said Madigan. She smiled coolly at her cousin.

Butter wouldn't melt in her mouth. It would catch fire.

Drgnan blushed.

Katie turned red.

Lily turned white.

Jasper looked around, confused.

The robot drove.

Madigan offered, "Come on down to my school, Drgnan Pghlik. I'll show you how New York's high society celebrates. We'll find you a tux. We'll ride in a limo."

The monk was startled and confused. "I— no. I wouldn't—couldn't—"

"Yes, you could," Madigan whispered to him.

"Excuse me," Katie demanded of Drgnan. "*Aren't* we going out?"

Drgnan's eyes were wide with surprise. "I am afraid I do not know exactly what that means."

"Oh," said Katie, "don't give me that monky-monk who-knows-what-is-real garbage!"

Madigan twirled a lock of her hair around her finger. She bragged, "The night of Snott Academy's annual dance, everyone in New York is jealous. Poor kids from across the city, and sad old people of twenty-five or thirty, all hate themselves and want to be *us* when they see how beautiful and glittering we all look—bright, adorable young things in love, heading through those golden doors into the annual Snott Ball."

Every head in the car turned toward her. Except the robot chauffeur.

"The . . . ," Drgnan said, "the Snott Ball? Your dance celebration, it is called the Snott Ball?"

She looked at him, wary. "Sure," she said. "That's what it's called. It's at Snott Academy. And it's an annual ball. Do you have a problem with that?"

Drgnan repeated, "The Snott Ball."

"Yeah. The Snott Ball."

Katie exclaimed, "The *SNOTBALL*? You're proud of the *SNOTBALL*?"

"I don't see what you find so funny about our delightfully decadent prom. It is attended by foreign princesses and child-dukes."

"The SNOTBALL!?!" said Katie.

Jasper was trying not to laugh. And Jasper did not always have much of a sense of humor. He and Drgnan were exchanging grins. Even Lily, who was worried about her mom, cracked a smile.

"Oh. My. Gosh," said Madigan. "I can't believe you losers would pooh-pooh the Snott Ball. And if you *laugh* at the fact that I said *pooh-pooh* in the same sentence as *Snott*, I am going to roll down the window and depressurize the cabin."

The Robo-Sedan flew back toward Pelt.

And the monster who awaited them there.

Just before the Robo-Sedan pulled into the driveway of Lily's house, they stopped for a moment right by the curb.

Lily pointed silently at her parents' bedroom window.

A weird green glow was reflected on the ceiling. It was two in the morning, and clearly the ghost was hovering above the bed like she had the night before.

Jasper said, "We can use the Astounding High-Pressure Holy Water Extruder Gun. When you knock and go in, Lily, your father and your possessed mother will probably come downstairs to see what's going on. Then I'll spray her with holy water and the ghost will have to leave."

Lily nodded. She blew her hair nervously out of her eyes.

The car pulled into the driveway and idled by the garage.

Craning their heads upward, the kids saw the green light flicker out.

A normal light turned on.

Lily's father must have heard the Robo-Sedan.

Lily and Jasper got out. Jasper had his Astounding High-Pressure Holy Water Extruder Gun in his arms still.

They went to the front door.

The other kids watched through the car windows.

Lily knocked, got out her key, turned the lock, and opened the door.

The house was dark except for a night-light at the top of the stairs. The night-light hurled shadows of the balusters down across the wall-to-wall carpet.

"Hello?" Lily called out softly. "Mom? Dad? I'm home."

And the creature that was supposed to be her mother appeared at the top of the stairs, grinning wickedly.

21

"DIE, FIEND FROM BEYOND!" Jasper roared, and sprayed Lily's possessed mother with holy water.

The fiend looked down to see herself drenched.

"It's swell to see you, too," said fake Mrs. Gefelty, brushing at the water on her arms with the bottom of her T-shirt. "Ow. Hey. Ow. That burns a little. So did you kids have a good time? Ow. Ow. Hey, Jasper, lovey-dove, could you stop that? With the squirt gun? It's a little peculiar and ungentlemanly."

Mr. Gefelty appeared on the staircase behind Mrs. G. "Jasper, what are you doing?" he said. "Stop that!"

"Mr. Gefelty," exclaimed Jasper, "that is *not your wife!*"

Mr. Gefelty and Mrs. Gefelty exchanged a look.

"Jasper," said Mr. Gefelty, coming downstairs and putting his hand on the Boy Technonaut's shoulder. "I know that Lily feels like something has happened to her mother. And I know you want to help her out. But I'm not sure that coming over here at two in the morning and squirting Mrs. Gefelty with a giant squirt gun is the answer. I'm not sure that it's a really normal thing to do."

"Desperate times call for desperate measures!" Jasper protested.

Mrs. Gefelty said, "Well, this desperate time is two in the morning. So why don't you pack your little self back into your automobile, you darling boy, and head home to slumberland?"

Frustrated, Jasper thrust the Astounding High-Pressure Holy Water Extruder Gun into

Lily's hands, stormed out of the house, and slammed the door.

Then he came back in, apologized for having slammed the door, and said politely, "Good night, Lily. Good night, Mr. Gefelty. Good night, Fake, Evil Mrs. Gefelty. I hope you all sleep well."

"Good night, Jasper," said Lily. "We'll talk tomorrow."

"Night, kid," said Mrs. Gefelty. "Sweet dreams." Jasper left.

Now Lily was alone with her unbelieving dad and her possessed mother.

"You go on to bed, Ben," Mrs. Gefelty said to her un-husband. "I want to have a little talk with Lily before she turns in."

"No!" said Lily.

"Lily, you're being ridiculous," said Mr. Gefelty. "Good night." He kissed his daughter on the head, walked up the stairs, gave his not-wife a cute little swat on the bottom, and headed off to bed.

Fake Mrs. Gefelty came down the stairs and sat on the lowest steps.

"Lily," she said, "sometimes it's difficult to understand what adults do. We lead lives that are so full of wild longing and romantic adventure, it's difficult for a girl to understand what throbs within us, once we're tall and gorgeous and successful."

Lily said, "You spent yesterday with Dad choosing which rolls of insulation in the basement should be thrown out."

"Oh, Lily, I've always lived my life on a grand scale."

Lily glared at the fake mother. "In Wanskuck, Rhode Island?"

That stopped her fake mother in her tracks. The ghost in the woman inspected her un-daughter.

"I see," said Vivian de NeVoshka. But it was with a kind of tired sadness that she said, "Let's go in the kitchen for some cocoa. Come along, Lils. You can show me where I put the match to light that microwave oven."

When Lily had furiously made them both instant hot cocoa, they sat at the kitchen table. Mrs. Gefelty curled her fingers around her cup. "I can't tell you how good it is to taste things again. Chocolate. Beets. Cheese. Anything." She blew on the cocoa. The tiny marshmallows spun. "It doesn't matter how long you live, or how hard life is sometimes, you always want to live more. You walk down the street in the spring, and all the trees are hung with blossoms, and there are people walking arm in arm through the city, through the cool streets, just beginning their lives—and you can't help but think, 'I want to start again. Why does this have to be over for me?'"

She gave a deep sigh and rammed her fingers like a comb into her hair. "How could I give up acting? How could I give up the stage? How could I give up the applause, the greasepaint, the gentleman callers? I couldn't. I just could not. So when I died, I decided I would return for another farewell tour. So for a few decades, I played the theater in Todburg as a ghost. I got stronger. But my talent—it was wasted out there in the boonies. The audiences were dead. And then a few nights ago, your mother came along. I decided that my train had finally arrived at the station, and that it was time for the late, great Vivian de NeVoshka to stage a revival, if you will."

Vivian de NeVoshka reached across the table with Mrs. Gefelty's hand and rubbed Lily's palm. "So we're just going to have to make the best of this difficult situation, Lily. Can you understand that? This is the acting challenge of my life! It's *tremendously* exhilarating. And there's the opportunity for us to make something wonderful out of the situation. If life gives you lemons, Lils, make lemonade.

"For example, we can talk about how to make you more glamorous. We can have girl-talks about things like boys. Within a few days,

I expect to see you on the arm of that handsome little monk. See? You savvy?"

"I don't *want* to talk about anything with you," said Lily.

Vivian shook her head. "I know what you're going through, Lily. But remember, this is not going to be easy for either of us. I have to learn to be a mother. And it's not easy to be a kind, gentle, understanding person when your actual mother is inside of me all the time, screaming hysterically for help. Right now, she's trying to get you to see her. She's been screaming without stop since the other day, silently, in the pit of our shared brain. It's not easy for me to talk calmly like this with all that going on. So you see, Lily, maybe you should think a bit less about your problems, and a bit more about what the rest of us are suffering." The actress took a sip of the cocoa. "I love warmth," she said. "For years, I didn't feel anything—anything hot, anything cold. That's one of the sad things about being a ghost. Ow. Ow. Please don't shoot me with that water gun, Lily. It kind of burns. Ow. Stop. Do I have to take the water gun away from you?"

The un-mother snarled, and for a moment, a green, hideous, decaying face flashed over Lily's mother's features. "It'll take more than a spritzer of holy water to get rid of me, kiddo." Then the green face sank back into the skin, and normal-looking Mrs. Gefelty leaned back in her chair. "I really never felt that one paltry lifetime was enough to explore my stage genius. When I lived and breathed, I never received the recognition I deserved. Do you know, Lily, I *created* the role of Sandy in Micah Retzblossom's *Sparrows of Autumn*?"

"I've never heard of it," Lily said quietly, miserably.

"It was an award-winning play."

Lily shrugged.

Vivian said, "It won the Bellbrook, Ohio, Best New Play of the Gourd Festival in 1934.

And did you know that I originated the role of Gertrude in *A Time to Spackle*?"

"I've never heard of it," Lily said, eager to hurt the monster's feelings.

"Bobbi Lee Hupp in *Dogs Die in the Sun*?"

"No."

"'Kitten-Lip' Watkins in the gangland thriller *Shoot First*?"

"No."

"The Enchantress Irina in Dame Lucy Potkins's *The Goblin Submersible*?"

"Nobody's ever heard of any of those plays," said Lily, relishing being rude. (It was unusual for her.)

Vivian insisted, "I am *someone*, Lily. You are lucky to have me in your *house*. Under your *roof*. I think you're a little immature to *understand* that, young woman. Listen: I was in the *moving pictures*."

Lily stared at her fake mother.

"It's true," said Vivian. "Spear-carrier number three in the silent hit *Penthesilea, Queen of the Amazons.* Oh, I looked a treat stalking through that jungle with my eyes rimmed in kohl. Ow. Ow. That hurts. Ow. I said stop it with the squirt gun, Lily. Stop. All right. I'm drawing the line. Ow. Stop. Off to bed! To your bedroom! Out! Go!"

And with that, the house settled down for the night.

Lily sat stewing in her room. For a long time, she sat sideways on her bed.

She reached into her pocket and pulled out a paper bag. She unscrunched the top and reached inside. Inside was the turquoise ankh. Her mother's gift to her, never given, found on a theater floor. Lily hung it around her neck. She rubbed the ankh with her thumbs. She frowned deeply and blew the hair out of her face.

Then she got up and went over to her computer. She began to search for books on ghosts and how to get rid of them.

And while she did that, in the master bed-room, Lily's fake mother silently rose and opened the window. Glowing green, she drifted out into the cold night.

She left the window open a crack for when she returned. But first, she had an errand to run.

The wind bore her away into the darkness.

22

The trees all over town moved restlessly in the November night-breezes. There was a constant, dark motion of thick pine elbows and dead, scorched branches.

At the Mulligans' house, Katie lay in her bed, worrying about Lily and her mom—but also near to tears because Drgnan had said he didn't know they were going out.

In the next room, Madigan lay in the guest bed. Her face was a terrifying, waxen white, and her eyes were dark holes. She lay motionless in the dark, with cracks running across the porcelain of her cheeks.

Oh, sorry. Just got a closer look. It's actually a layer of white chocolate cosmetic toning mask. The dark around the eyes is a silk sleeping visor. She's fine, and she'll wake up with really moist skin.

At the Dashes' ultramodern house of the future, Drgnan lay in the guest bedroom. So he could sleep like a monk (which means uncomfortably), he and Jasper had dragged the mattress over and leaned it up against the wall. Instead Drgnan lay on a bed of sharp gravel. He snored slightly, dreaming of saints.

Jasper was asleep too, in his futuristic bed. Lights from projects gently blinked and lit wires, panels, and levers. He stirred, as if he could sense, even through his dreams, that someone was entering the room.

Someone was walking across the floor toward him.

Bare feet sank silently into the thick carpet.

Jasper shifted his arms near his chin. Winked awake. The machines lit his hands and his blankets.

Jasper did not hear a thing. He shoved groggily at his pillow to plump it. He scratched his neck with his thumb. Turned over.

And saw his mother looming over him.

She had thrown on a quilted brunch coat hastily over her nightgown. "Jasper," whispered Dolores Dash. "Jasper, honey! I think someone is outside, trying to get in."

Jasper was up like a shot. He ran to his desk and rummaged in a drawer. "It might not do any good, if it's a ghost," he whispered back, "but I'll feel safer with my ray gun."

They crept out into the hall.

The ultramodern house was dark. On different levels, by balconies and floating staircases, the huge plate-glass windows showed nothing but black. Something could easily be looking in from outside, out in the night.

"I heard it in my bedroom," said Mrs. Dash.

They listened to the sound of the wind against concrete.

Jasper, in his striped pajamas, walked carefully toward Mrs. Dash's room. He held the ray gun at the ready, wishing he had kept the prototype of the Astounding High-Pressure Holy Water Extruder Gun. This was one instance where water might be more powerful than lasers.

He opened the door to his mother's room and stalked in. It was dark. It was freezing. He flipped on the light.

One window was open. The wintry breeze came in.

Jasper felt fear drop in the pit of his stomach. He walked toward the window. The curtains blew as if someone was there, shaking them. Jasper held up his ray gun. He stepped around the corner of the bed.

And saw, sprawled on the floor, Mrs. Gefelty. As if she'd tumbled in from the outdoors.

"Great Scott!" he exclaimed.

And his mother's voice behind him said, "No, over here. Behind you."

He swiveled.

His own mother stood right behind him, grinning like a psychopath, licked with green fire.

He barked with horror. *"Mom!"*

Mrs. Dash's body pointed at Mrs. Gefelty. Mrs. Gefelty was out cold, unconscious. Jasper's mother explained, "I left her for a minute. I thought I'd do a little visiting here. Pay a call." She looked around. "You have any cigarettes in this dump?"

Jasper stumbled. He pointed the ray gun. "Get—get away! Get out of her! Get out of her, I say!"

Fake Mrs. Dash smiled at him. "Go ahead, kiddo. Shoot. Shoot me. Try it. Pull the trigger."

Jasper was horrified. There was nothing he could do. Anything he did to hurt the ghost would hurt his own beloved mother more.

The actress reached out and took the ray gun out of his fingers. She tossed it on the bed.

"Now," she said. "Let's review a few things. We all are going to have to get along. That may be difficult for you, but you'd better give it a shot or someone you love will get hurt. Here's the arrangement: You're not going to let Mr. Gefelty know what's going on. You're not going to tell Lily you think she's right, and that I'm a ghost. If you try to dislodge me from Mrs. Gefelty, I'm going to come after your mother. Okeydokey? Think of it like this: We've all got roles to play. We're all acting. Stick with your lines, kiddo. You go off-script, and I'm going to make a casting substitution. You savvy?"

Jasper didn't answer. He just stared in horror.

The woman who was usually his mother nodded, winked, and knelt down by Mrs. Gefelty. She gripped Mrs. Gefelty's wrist.

Mrs. Gefelty moved uncomfortably. Her eyes started to open. She saw Jasper's mother. She moaned. She was about to speak, about to whisper something to her friend.

Then Mrs. Dash's eyes rolled up into her head and she collapsed. And a green light shot across the surface of Mrs. Gefelty's skin.

Then Mrs. Gefelty rose unsteadily. She

brushed herself off. She moved with certainty, like someone who was long accustomed to being onstage.

"So long," she said. "Sleep tight."

She climbed up on the windowsill and leaped. Jasper saw her blow away on the wind.

He sat on his mother's bed.

On the floor, his mother began to come back to herself. She said she'd had a terrible dream.

23

There is never good weather in horror novels. When a madman with a hook for a hand breaks out of the asylum, it is never sunny with a high in the upper seventies. When a vampire rages through a Gothic house, trying to pry off the doorknob of the closet where you're hiding, it is very rarely comfortable shirtsleeve weather. It is never just slightly cloudy when a race of flesh-eating grubs in the sewers grows to the size of bulldogs and bursts out of city toilets. No, at the beginning of a horror novel, you might get one scene of children playing innocently on a lawn with Technicolor green grass and a blue, blue sky above them—but you know that it's not going to last. The bright, jolly colors just mean disaster and mountain-goblins are on their way. So listen, pal, don't get out your tanning butter. You are in for rain, rain, and more rain. Incoming low-pressure systems. A 100 percent chance of monstershowers.

It was raining again when our heroes met for lunch at Jasper's Astounding Aero-Bistro. The Aero-Bistro was a nice floating restaurant Jasper had riveted together some years before, and had appeared in such books as *Jasper Dash and the Side Dish from Saturn* and *Whales on Stilts!* In this lovely, airborne bistro, you could sip frappés and eat chocolate cheesecake, served by robot waiters, while floating above a scenic gorge near Pelt. Katie, Jasper, Lily, Drgnan, and Madigan had met there to have a powwow about how to deal with their dummy mummy mommy problem.

Madigan, needless to say, did not want to be there. She *had* to go because Katie was going, and Mrs. Mulligan insisted that the two girls go everywhere together. Madigan was determined to make everyone know how bored she was. She sighed and looked out at the sheets of rain blowing across the gorge. She rattled her ice-cream spoon against her teeth. She glared at the lights of the harbor in the distance. The only thing she liked about sitting in a flying restaurant was that she got great reception for her iSquawk.

Katie herself did not necessarily want to be there either. She wanted to help Lily any way she could, but she wasn't very interested in seeing Drgnan Pghlik just then. She was ignoring him, in fact. She pretended that she didn't hear or see him.

When Jasper arrived with Drgnan, Katie turned away from Drgnan and said to the Boy Technonaut, "Too bad you came alone."

"I didn't," said Jasper. "Drgnan is right here."

"Sitting by yourself in the Robo-Sedan, it must've gotten pretty lonely."

"Katie," Jasper insisted, "Drgnan is right h—

Great Scott! Drgnan must be invisible to you!"

"Jasper," said Lily quietly, "I think maybe Katie is—"

"Possessed by a monster?" Jasper pulled out his ray gun.

Katie rolled her eyes and stormed off to their table.

"I believe that she harbors anger within her," said Drgnan miserably.

Jasper looked a little confused, but he stashed his gun nonetheless, not wanting to panic the ice-cream social crowd.

They went and sat. At first it was very uncomfortable. Madigan kept typing things they couldn't see. She apparently no longer had a crush on Drgnan, now that he'd made fun of the Snott Ball. Meanwhile, Drgnan tried to be extra nice to Katie, who still pretended not to hear him.

When the food came, they began to discuss the situation.

Jasper said, "The ghost took over my mother

last night. Lily, your mother flew to our house. I mean, your fake, haunted mother. She threatened me."

Lily turned pale. Katie exclaimed, "That's terrible, Jas! Terrible!"

Jasper set his mouth grimly. "A threat to Dash is nothing but an invitation to action. It just convinced me we have got to solve this problem now—because otherwise, Vivian de NeVoshka will only become more dangerous to our families." Concerned, he asked Lily, "How are things at your house?"

"Terrible," said Lily. "She was doing show tunes all morning in the shower." Lily made fists and laid them on the table. "When I came down to breakfast, she sang 'I Wanna Be Loved by You, Boop-boop-be-doo.'"

"Super ick," Katie said. "So what are we going to do?"

"I think I have a plan," said Lily, hunching her back and leaning toward her friends. "Last night I looked at some old books about ghost hunting. Books from the 1600s."

Jasper asked, "Why, Lily, where did you find them?" He was clearly impressed. "Some musty library with bats in the eaves and grimoires shackled to the desks?"

"A monastic labyrinth of ancient learning?" Drgnan suggested.

Lily shrugged shyly. "No, you can find it all online now. All these books have been scanned in. Here, look. I printed out some pages."

Madigan laughed out loud richly. Then she stopped herself and looked around the table. "Oh, sorry," she said. "It was just something Aaron wrote. He is *so* totes naughty." She dropped her gaze back to her iSquawk and kept typing.

Lily slid some pages across the table to her friends. They had old woodcuts on them of magicians in long robes.

"Look at this one," Lily said. She pointed. "It's from something called . . .

Anti-phantasmata

YE HISTORIE OF YE GHOST-SMACKER.

"It's by a guy who hunted ghosts in England. Here's what he says about getting them out of people.

Ye most mighty and powerful ghosts and spirites can, by the touching of a person, and gripping onto that person for some time, enter into that person's minde, and make them walk about and speake, like unto a puppet. Such spirites can only be caste out with a greate amount of holie water, suffcient to bathe them. When these terrible spirites leave the bodie which they have infested, they will seize upon another, and make a strong attempt to controul that new person, UNLESS you do caste out the spirit inside a Magick Circle. A ghost without a bodie cannot leave such a circle. So long as there is no other living being within ye magick circle, ye ghost will not be able to escape, but shall be trapped by ye sorcerous symbols and runic devices. It can then be bottled or jugged by the following methode. . . .

"He gives all kinds of instructions for making the magic circle and for putting the ghost into a jar. See? Here's a diagram."

"So what we need to do," Jasper mused, "is find a way to drench your fake mother with holy water . . ."

"Inside one of these magic circles," said Drgnan.

"I'm sorry," said Katie. "I didn't hear that last thing. It sounded like a breeze blew past." She gestured to where the rain beat against the windows.

"Katie . . . ," Drgnan pleaded.

"Sometimes the wind," mused Katie, "almost seems to say someone's name."

Lily looked back and forth between Katie and Drgnan. She said, "Um, I have a plan. I have a way to lure my mother—I mean, the ghost—into a magic circle. But it's going to be kind of dangerous. Because if we screw up, she'll be able to jump into one of us."

Lightning lit the restaurant. A thunderclap

rattled the dishes on the tables. Diners looked up from their dinners.

Drgnan said, "Danger is sometimes necessary. The turtle must put its head outside its shell, if it is to feast upon leaves."

Katie rolled her eyes. "The turtle," she muttered. "We're talking about Lily's *mother*, Drgnan, not a turtle." She got up and walked over to a window. She stared out into the slashing rain, arms crossed.

Drgnan looked at his half-finished cheesecake.

Jasper said, "At least she heard you."

Drgnan got up and went over to talk to her.

Jasper called after him, "Hey-up, Drg! Will you want the rest of your cheesecake?"

Katie was watching the cars crawl along the roads down below. Drgnan stood by her side.

"I'm sorry, Katie. I didn't know what you meant . . . when you asked me to the dance."

"And held hands with me," she reminded him bitterly.

"I've lived all of my life in a monastery on top of a mountain. You know we are not allowed to go on dates."

"Well, that's a stupid rule. And you're stupid to not get what was going on. Do you realize how—how *embarrassing* this is?"

Lightning cracked down from the sky, distantly. They could see its whole broken length, cloud to ground.

"When the stingray lays its eggs, it cannot—"

"Oh, shut up," said Katie, and walked away.

Drgnan blinked, stunned. He rested himself on the brass window frame. He stared out into the storm.

After a while, Lily came over to him. "Don't worry," she said. "Katie gets mad really easy, but she also forgets really easy to be mad."

Drgnan nodded slightly. "Thank you, Lily," he said. "I am sorry that I misled her. I did not mean to. That would be a wicked thing to do. I have pledged never to tell a lie."

He and Lily watched the rain fall.

"Jasper and I have worked out a plan," said Lily. "We know what we're going to do."

Drgnan smiled. "That makes my heart joyful," he said. "Action is better than rest."

Lily pressed her fingers up against the glass. It felt cold from the water that sloshed against the other side. "You're going to have to go back soon, aren't you? To Vbngoom?"

He didn't seem happy about it. "The, um, swallow must return to its nest," he said.

Lily twisted her mouth and then blew her hair up out of her eyes. "I'm going to miss you," she told him. "It's good to have someone to talk to about some things."

Drgnan said, "I will miss you, too." With some difficulty, he started to say something, and then stopped. Then started. Then stopped. Then, finally, said, "If I were permitted to 'go out' with anyone, it would be—"

Yeah, this scene might have ended

very romantically, if the Aero-Bistro hadn't been struck by lightning right then. There was a huge crash, and the floor shook. The whole thing lit up like a pinball machine, and then everything went dark, and all the diners started screaming and running around, worried that the restaurant was about to crash down out of the sky.

Oh, Lily waited for the end of Drgnan's sentence—waited with incredible longing—as robots shuffled everyone into aerial life rafts and sent them drifting off toward the earth.

But she was in a different lifeboat than Drgnan.

And by the time they all touched down in the parking lot, and crawled out of the lifeboats with helmets on their heads and giant inflat-able rings around their middles, and the police came and made sure everyone was all right, and the news cameras began rolling, the romantic moment had passed. From across the parking lot, Drgnan just called, "See you tomorrow, Lily!" He grinned at her.

By which he meant: See you tomorrow—
when we put the *master plan* into action!

The plan that would either free Lily's
mother entirely—or set the ghost free to attack
them all.

24

"Well, I call it real neighborly for Mrs. Dash to invite us over for a pool party!" exclaimed fake Mrs. Gefelty. She adjusted her giant-brimmed sun hat. Outside the car, the rain poured down.

(Horror novel. So, still raining.)

"It's kind of a Jacuzzi," said Lily. "Or a hot tub or something. She and Jasper thought it would cheer us all up, since the weather's been so bad recently."

Fake Mrs. Gefelty reached into the backseat to stroke Lily's cheek. "Honey," she said, "I think it's great that you're coming around. Are we friends again?"

Mr. Gefelty smiled in the driver's seat.

Lily had cleverly pretended that she was

trying to live in peace with her ghost mother. She'd gotten fake phantom Mrs. Gefelty interested in the party by saying that it was a time for them all to do something together, so they'd be more like a family.

Jasper Dash had a space-age hot tub inside his house, surrounded by glass, in a kind of cube that stuck out of the basement. That way, on starry nights, Mrs. Dash could take a martini down and drink it in the bubbling water while she looked up at the Milky Way above her and dreamed of spacemen.

Mrs. Dash did not use it much anymore. It was getting old and cracked. Usually, it was filled with chemicals while Jasper did experiments.*

But for this occasion, he and Drgnan had cleaned the hot tub and filled it up to the brim . . . with holy water.

---

*This resulted in some unfortunate mix-ups, when Mrs. Dash mistook the boiling chemicals for bubbling warm water. For details, see *Jasper Dash and the Invisible Skin*, *Jasper Dash and His Startling Antigravity Mother*, etc.

I think you see where this is going.

When the Gefeltys arrived, Jasper was standing by the door to the garage, flipping burgers on the grill. He waved his spatula. They went right in, bundling their towels and their salad in their arms.

So far, so good.

But let's stop for a minute here. I might as well tell you a little secret known to thriller writers and action hacks like myself: If there's a plan in a book—a secret plan, like dousing your ghost-possessed mother in a Jacuzzi of holy water—and if it's going to work out right, then you *don't tell readers about the plan ahead of time.* Because the fun is seeing the plan unfold.

But if, on the other hand, you as an author know that the plan *isn't* going to work out the way the characters suspect, if you know there are going to be problems and unforeseen tangles and crazy goofs, then you *do* tell the readers about the plan ahead of time—because then they'll be surprised when something goes wrong.

So if muscle-hunk Dunk Wingaard, in his action movie *Curse of the Jaguar III*, is going to raid the enemy's lair, and he shows the audience the whole map and the wiring layout before the attack, and you see him telling all his fellow commandos their duties, then probably—*probably*—you know he's in for a much rougher ride than he knows. (Knife pits; hidden cameras; snake guns.) He will have forgotten *one little thing*—and that will make all the difference. (Usually, as the clock on the bomb counts down toward exploding.)

Now what does this simple rule of action mean in this situation?

Well, I've let the plan slip: holy water in the hot tub.

So something is going to go wrong.

Very, very wrong.

It's going to be awful.

Just watch and see.

25

There's nothing that can go wrong now, thought Jasper Dash, Boy Technonaut.

Jasper smirked as he flipped the burgers. Everything was set. Earlier that day, while a garden hose filled the Jacuzzi with holy water, Jasper and Drgnan had drawn the magic circle from Lily's book around the hot tub. It was a chalk double ring filled with mystical symbols. Then they had hid the chalk circle with big ferns and flowering plants both inside and outside the rings—taking care to let nothing cross the lines. If anything broke that circle when the ghost was forced out of Mrs. Gefelty, it would be able to escape. If any other living thing was inside the circle when the ghost left

Lily's mom, it would be able to jump into a new body. So they were careful how they drew the diagram, and very careful in how they arranged the plants.

Then they had gone out and bought frozen party pizza bites.

Now candles were lit all around the hidden magic circle, reflecting off the fronds of the ferns and the bubbles in the hot tub. Everyone was at the house. Everything was in place.

Jasper grinned just thinking about what that awful ghost was in for.

His mother appeared in her bathing suit and espadrilles, carrying a plate of marinated chicken pieces. "Everything set, Jas?" she asked.

"Just a few more minutes," Jasper said. "I think these are about ready."

Mrs. Dash slid the tray of uncooked chicken onto a workbench. "That's great, honey. Could you cook these, too? Mr. Mulligan loves some chicken."

"Certainly, Mother," said Jasper.

"I hope nothing goes wrong. I want this to be a swell party."

Jasper smiled to himself. "Don't worry, Mother," he said. "Nothing will go wrong."

"Do you mean that in a general sense, kiddo," his mother asked, "or are you referring specifically to some wacky plot you have to throw me out of Mrs. Gefelty's body?"

Jasper looked up, startled.

His mother winked at him. "I just thought I'd borrow your mumsy for a test-drive. Just to remind you of our little agreement." She reached out and grabbed some of Jasper's cheek and shook it. "I'd better get back inside. Mrs. Gefelty might wake up soon."

She turned and walked back across the garage, into the house.

Jasper watched her go, mouth open in shock.

26

Inside, it was awkward. Mrs. Dash had gone off to talk to Jasper. Mrs. Gefelty had apparently fallen asleep on the couch almost as soon as everyone got there. And Drgnan had decided that it fell to him to be the host for the moment, so he was trying to keep everyone happy— while Katie refused to recognize that he actually existed.

"Can I get anyone some more soda?" he asked.

"Can the wind offer soda?" Katie mused. "Can soda blow in the breezes?"

Drgnan cleared his throat and held up a platter. "Or some of these party pizzas? Mrs. Mulligan?"

"Thanks, Drgnan," said Mrs. Mulligan. She took one.

"Mom!" said Katie. "Where did you get that party pizza? It must have fluttered in like a pepperoni butterfly and settled on your hand."

"Katie," said her father, who was on the police force and kind of no-nonsense, "are you always going to act this weird at parties? Because if so, from now on you can stay at home working on your rug hooking."

Madigan had given up on this conversation entirely. She was off in the dining room, doing her Pilates exercise routine by the windows.

Mrs. Dash came in and sat next to Mrs. Gefelty. "So. We have some catching up to do," she said, seizing her unconscious friend's hand.

There was a small green spark between their fingers.

Suddenly Mrs. Dash's eyes rolled up in her head. She slumped backward. Mrs. Gefelty woke up abruptly, smiled, and stood. "Well, how is everyone? Is the party getting a glow on?"

"I was just offering everyone some party pizzas, Mrs. Gefelty," said Drgnan.

"What a perfect little gentleman," said Mrs. Gefelty, and winked at Lily.

"I don't know who you hear," said Katie, sitting on the arm of a love seat, facing away from the monk. "I don't hear anyone at all, except the frying of fat in the fryolator."

Drgnan's mouth dropped open as he remembered, "Fryolator! The deep-fried Sheep-Butter Bars!" He scrambled to the kitchen to scum off the oil.

Fake Mrs. Gefelty had been watching Katie and Drgnan closely. She had been noticing that the two were arguing. Seeing this, Lily decided to make her move.

Lily said to her un-mother, "Could we talk? About, you know, private stuff, for a second?"

Fake Mrs. Gefelty looked delighted. She said to the other adults, "Motherhood!" and threw up her hands, as if to say, *These crazy kids! Asking my advice all the time!* "Sure, Lily.

What say we step into another room? Excuse us, people."

Lily looked around at everyone.

Now was the time. She searched each face. All the people she loved. If something went wrong, she might be seeing them now for the last time.

"Let's go in here," she said, and pointed through the sliding doors at the room with the candles and the hot tub.

"Sure, kiddo," said fake Mrs. Gefelty, and she gestured for Lily to lead.

Lily stood up. She reached into her hoodie. She pulled out the turquoise ankh, symbol of life eternal, which her mom had meant to give her, and she held on to it with one hand. Wherever her mother actually was at this point, Lily hoped she could see them and was watching over it all.

Lily and her fake, undead mother went into the hot-tub room and slid the door closed behind them.

Mr. Mulligan was telling everyone an insane story about how people had filed police reports about a woman in pajamas flying over the neighborhood the night before.

But Katie wasn't listening. She was watching what was happening through the glass doors to make sure that Lily was safe.

Lily wasn't.

27

Lily and her ghost-possessed mother sat by the softly bubbling tub, which was sunk into the concrete floor. The horror-novel rain fell hard against the windows, but inside that chamber, it felt warm and tropical. The plants made the glassy room green. The candles flickered, spaced around the cauldron of holy water.

"It's about the monk boy, isn't it?" said fake Mrs. Gefelty. "I can tell you do love that pint-size Saint Francis something awful."

"I don't know what to do," said Lily. "It seems impossible that anything will ever work out. My best friend thought she was going out with him, and—and—he's going to be leaving soon, going back to his monastery. And he's not supposed to go out with anyone anyway, because he's a monk." Lily was pretending to want her ghost-mother's advice, and in fact, acting upset wasn't very difficult. She was actually miserable about Drgnan leaving.

But her tears were not real. She just scrunched up her face.

"Oh, Lils. Lils, come on! If the sun doesn't come out and dry up those clouds, no one's going to want to picnic with you."

Lily, in pretend sorrow, put her arm around her un-mother.

Fake Mrs. Gefelty looked confused for a second—never having had an actual daughter, even one who was just pretending to have a crisis. Then she leaned down to kiss her on the head.

"You know," said fake Mrs. Gefelty, "when I was on the stage, there was something people used to say: The one thing no man can stand up against is a—"

For an instant, Lily hesitated before pushing

her mother into the pool. For an instant, all this fakeness looked almost like realness to Lily—the face of her beloved mother, and her own sadness about Drgnan living so far away—but then she remembered her mother lost and screaming somewhere inside the ghost's vicious, jealous heart—and she shoved.

Her un-mother was already bent over to kiss her, and went in easily, toppling, yelping.

Those yelps became more desperate when she felt that the water was holy water. "LILY!" she yelled. "LILY! DON'T!"

"Where's my mother?" Lily demanded. (She was not used to demanding . . . and strangely, the thing that gave her courage now was fear.)

Green sparks zapped up and down Mrs. Gefelty's body wherever the water sploshed and splashed. Mrs. Gefelty writhed and slapped, trying to grab the concrete edge of the tub.

Lily sprinted several steps back. She got herself outside the magic circle.

Now the ghost would be unjoined from

her mother's body. A few seconds after that, if there was no other host for the ghost to move into, it would evaporate into thin air—Vivian de NeVoshka would move on to the next world.

It was now like there were two people struggling there: solid Mrs. Gefelty and the specter, translucent, with blats of green flame shooting out from its joints and its eyes.

The sliding doors slammed open, and the others ran in.

"Save her!" the adults yelled. "What's happening to her?"—"She's being electrocuted!"

"Don't!" said Katie. "It's a ghost! It's being thrown out of Mrs. Gefelty!"

The spirit was losing, weakened by the shocks of blessed water. It was peeling away from Mrs. Gefelty. It had a withered face, and long, lank, silver hair, and dead holes for eyes, and a torn mouth that, at the merest suggestion, would gladly burst into tunes from *Guys and Dolls* or *Annie Get Your Gun*.

Mr. Gefelty ran forward, hollering Mrs.

Gefelty's name—and Lily grabbed his arm. "Don't, Dad! Don't! Don't go inside the magic circle! The ghost will get you!"

He demanded, "Out of my way! Lily! OUT OF MY WAY!"

Then, suddenly, Mrs. Gefelty collapsed, facedown, on the side of the pool, and everyone, adults and kids, could see the ghost floating above the vapors of the water. An actress of green steam with an evil glint in her eye. She surveyed them and shot toward Lily, claws outstretched.

And slammed up against the wall of the magic circle with a clang. She struggled against it, smacking at the invisible barrier with her palms.

"I can't—can't come to my end this way," she wailed. "Beating at nonexistent walls like a common street mime! No! The show . . . the show *must go on!*"

Now that Lily saw how desperate the woman was to live, she felt sorry for hurling her into the vat of holy water. A little sorry. But then she remembered her own trapped mother, who was breathing heavily, arms sprawled across the concrete, drenched with holy water.

The ghost flashed back over to Mrs. Gefelty and surveyed her. Too much holy water soaking the body. But Vivian de NeVoshka was fading. The magic circle was taking its toll. She was becoming more and more see-through. Soon she wouldn't be there at all.

"I'm calling an ambulance," said Bick Mulligan. He dialed 9-1-1.

Groggy Mrs. Gefelty lifted up her head. She smiled at Lily.

"Come on!" Lily's dad urged. "Get out of there!"

Lily stepped forward. "No, Mom! Don't get out! Stay in the water! Keep in the holy water! She's going to be gone soon!"

And so the ghost would have been.

If an Adirondack tarantula who'd been

hiding behind one of the potted plants hadn't toddled out next to the hot tub right then.

The tarantula was not in a good mood. In the last few days, he had been kicked, thrown through the air, locked in a bathroom, and had clung onto the bottom of a flying Robo-Sedan for several hours. This was it. He had traveled a long, long way to finally bite that stupid woman who'd originally bashed him up in the car. He really could not stand that woman. And there she was, slumped by the water. Now he was finally going to take a chomp out of her.

He scuttled across the floor.

And suddenly started dreaming of show business.

28

Horrified, the crowd of kids and adults saw the ghost shoot down and embrace the tarantula. They saw the tarantula pause. They saw the ghost spill into the spider like backward smoke from a swallowed fire.

"Oh no!" Katie said. "The tarantula is possessed!"

Jasper Dash, Boy Technonaut, pulled out his ray gun and aimed it at the spider.

"Don't kill it!" Drgnan protested. "It's just a hapless tarantula!"

Lily agreed. "And it's furry!"

They exchanged a look. There were so many things they agreed about.

"Mrs. Gefelty!" said Katie. "Wake up!

Wake up! You have to throw the tarantula into the hot tub with you! *Grab the tarantula, Mrs. Gefelty!*"

Mrs. Gefelty stirred, but she was not fully awake. And I have to say, if you are ever awakened out of a long, weird dream by someone telling you, "You have to throw that tarantula into the hot tub with you!" you might pause a second to consider the situation. For example, you might ask yourself, *Am I really awake? You might ask yourself, What hot tub? And, for that matter, what tarantula? And actually, is this really a great piece of advice?*

The tarantula turned with glowing green eyes and began to skitter toward the crowd. Vivian de NeVoshka, driving the spider, was going to rush across the line of the magic circle and escape while she had the chance!

Mrs. Gefelty moaned. She raised her head up and blinked.

"The spider!" Lily said. "Grab the spider!"

Mrs. Gefelty saw the tarantula, but it was

moving too quickly. She stretched her arm out feebly—couldn't reach the spider.

It was about to step across the line—and the ghost would be free!

Until Madigan Westlake-Duvet sauntered out from behind them and broke the magic circle herself, accidentally kicking the spider across the room with the toe of her David Brunwerfer "Malibu" cork wedgie.

Madigan was wearing a cherry red bikini by Santro Pay. She was carrying a towel. And she was going to sit and relax in the hot tub.

The tarantula picked itself up and shook itself off.

"Madigan!" screamed Katie. "No! Madigan! Get out of the magic circle! Run!"

"Hello? We came over to use the hot tub. So use the hot tub I'm gunna."

The tarantula made a beeline for the New York bathing beauty.

"RUN!" Katie repeated. "GET OUT OF THERE, YOU JERK!"

"Listen," said Madigan. "I heard someone call an ambulance. If you think I'm going to miss the opportunity when the paramedics get here, possibly with the handsome, green-eyed son of one of them who's traveling along with his surgeon father because he's thinking about going into neurosurgery when he grows up, and then he walks in, and there I am, lying by this hot tub in this bathing suit, then, um, yeah, you have another think coming. So. Any other objections?"

Lily said, *"There's a ghost in the form of a tarantula and it's going to get you!"*

Which would be enough to worry most people.

But Madigan sighed, looked at Lily, and had just enough time to say, "Oh my gosh, you are such a loser. Do you hear what you're *saying*? I know it's hard for you to understand, because you're wearing that completely shapeless, unbecoming hoodie, and you couldn't really pull off a totes hot Santro Pay bikini like me, but when

you wear something like this, you want people to—"

Then the tarantula got to her. It wrapped its legs around her foot.

There was a spark of green near her heel.

She opened her eyes in surprise. She wobbled on her David Brunwerfer wedgies.

"No!" said Mrs. Mulligan. "Katie! Do something! Save your cousin!"

Katie looked around for a solution—any solution. Lamely, she said, "Mrs. Gefelty . . . Mrs. Gefelty, could you throw that girl near you into the hot tub?"

Mrs. Gefelty looked around in bewilderment.

The girl blinked as if just awakening.

"Madigan?" said Mrs. Mulligan. "Come this way. Come on. Quickly."

"NO!" said Katie. "Stay where you are! Stay inside the circle!"

Mrs. Mulligan protested, "But she's—"

"It's *not really her, Mom!*" Katie cried.

And Madigan Westlake-Duvet grinned. She cackled wildly. "Here I am! It's so good—so good to be young again!" She danced a few steps and made jazz hands.

"Saints alive!" swore Drgnan. "How are we going to get her out of Madigan?"

"You'll never pry me loose from this piece of prime real estate!" Vivian de NeVoshka growled from the mouth of the haunted it-girl.

Lily was frantic. This was a disaster. They had succeeded in dislodging the specter from her mother—only to get her jammed in Madigan. They were responsible for that girl being possessed—controlled by a snarling, furious, jealous spirit! Lily had no idea how to get the ghost out of the girl.

Madigan howled with laughter and danced from foot to foot, knees high. She hugged herself and flung her arms around.

"Oh no," said Mrs. Mulligan. "Oh no, no, no." What would her sister, Madigan's mother, say?

Madigan began walking toward them. She stuck her toe across the magic circle and wiggled it. "Oooh!" she said. "Big powerful magic circle. You can't stop me now!" She jumped across. "Ha, ha! Here I am!" She danced a few jazz squares back and forth across the magical barrier.

Then she reached out and snapped Katie on the nose.

Drgnan tried to grab her.

The haunted Manhattanite shoved Drgnan out of the way and walked into the living room. She picked up a Diet Dr. Pepper and snapped the top. She took a long swallow, smacked her lips with delight, and grinned ghoulishly at the horrified families.

"So," said Madigan. "You yanked me out of Lily's mother. But you're not getting me out of this kid. I'm here to stay. Vivian de NeVoshka never falls for the same chump-stunt twice."

This was terrible. Mrs. Mulligan made an awful, terrified whiny noise in her throat. Jasper looked frantically around the room, but there were no gadgets that could solve this problem. Drgnan bit his lip.

"What are we going to do?" Lily bleated. "How are we going to save Madigan?"

And then Katie looked around slyly. "You know," she said. "We could . . ."

"Oh, swell," said the ghost-girl. "This should be just dandy." She put the can to her lips and raised it high above them, so a long arc of brown soda shot through the air and right down her gullet.

Politely, Katie continued, "I think you're asking the wrong question, Lily. It's not *how* do we save Madigan. It's *why do we have to*?"

Everyone looked at Katie in horror.

Katie held up her hands defensively. "Just listen! Just listen! Nobody actually *liked* Madigan. Maybe she'd be a better person if she was controlled by an undead actress from Rhode Island."

"French-occupied Russia," snapped Vivian. "Or Russian-occupied France."

Mrs. Mulligan scolded her daughter, "Katie, that's an awful thing to say about your cousin! Of course people love Madigan. I mean, her mother does, for instance. Her mother . . . Well, her mother doesn't exactly *love* her, but they're very *friendly* with each other. Sometimes." She looked at her husband. "Back me up here, Bick. We can't just send Madigan back to New York possessed by a dead person."

"No, Mrs. Mulligan," said Vivian. "You can. One second." Madigan's lovely face went through a weird change—her eyes closed and popped open—and she said, "Hello? Could someone ask me what *I* want to do for once? This is Madigan. Vivian is letting me drive for a second. Okay, listen, this is going to work out great. Vivian tells me she's going to make me a star. We're going to act on Broadway. We're going to be the toast of New York."

"Really?" said Lily. "You don't mind having two people in your head?"

Katie muttered, "There was a lot of empty room in there to begin with."

"*Ac*-tually," said Madigan, setting down her diet soda and slinging her towel over her shoulder, "this is the best social thing that's happened to me all year. I've always wanted a very special best friend. You know, a BFF. And who could be a better best friend forever than myself? I already totes love me. I know I'm the only person who's as cool as me. So now I can always hang out with myself, and go places with myself, and double-date boys with myself, and I won't have to put up with Keds-wearing losers like you."

She walked into the center of the living room and struck a pose. "Is there a piano in this dump?" she asked in the voice of Vivian de NeVoshka. "Because we're in the mood to sing a duet."

Thankfully, there was not.

29

After the unquiet spirit took over Madigan Westlake-Duvet, it actually turned out to be a pretty cool party. Mr. Gefelty went down to the garage and brought in the chicken and burgers Jasper had cooked. For Drgnan, Mrs. Dash had whipped up a platter of twigs and fried locusts. He picked up a birch stick and began peeling off the white bark with his teeth. He exclaimed, "This is great, Mrs. D!" Madigan/Vivian went off to iSquawk her New York friends and brag about her new dual personality. The spider, a little dazed, wandered down to the basement and found a super supply of flies. And after the smoke cleared, Lily and Jasper, kind of without planning it, started using spatulas quietly to flip a piece of crumpled aluminum foil back and forth over the couch. It became a game. Mrs. Dash gasped at the thought of what might happen to her upholstery, but she was too happy to scold them.

After a while, Katie clearly wanted to play the aluminum game, but she didn't want to look like she was having fun in front of Drgnan. She wanted Drgnan to know she was still mad. And Drgnan didn't want to look like he was having fun in front of Katie. But they both wanted to pick up the big wooden salad forks and join in for a game of doubles.

Finally they couldn't stop themselves. After all, Drgnan wouldn't be around forever. Another few days, and he'd be heading back to his monastery in the mountains of Delaware. Shyly, they both grabbed wooden salad forks and joined opposite teams. The aluminum foil flashed through the air. There were heroic saves.

Lily, as it turned out, was a little better at tinfoil-flipping than at basketball. She and Drgnan made a good team.

They smiled at each other and missed a serve.

Lily's mother, restored to consciousness, just sat and watched them play their tinfoil game. She was too happy to speak.*

I should mention, in passing, that Madigan was much less of a pain in the neck once she was possessed. For one thing, her visit was over soon, and she went back to New York. She and Vivian tried out for plays. They were an awful actress, but that never stopped anyone. Soon the *New York Post* ran a piece on Madigan and her ghost, and then everyone in Manhattan wanted to be possessed. They all flocked up to Todburg. Soon the theater on Midnight Boulevard was doing a great business with the tourists, and Main Street was hopping with little art shops and cafés that sold bran-nut muffins and brioche. The locals who were actually still alive weren't always happy with this—they said the tide of wealthy New Yorkers was much more irritating than

---

*See page 43. I don't welsh on my promises.

a small-town zombie apocalypse—but all the *dead* citizens of Todburg were having the time of their lives, er, I mean deaths.

For our heroes—Jasper, Lily, Katie, and Drgnan—there were simpler pleasures than being possessed by undead nineteenth-century cattle farmers. At the party, they ran up and down the stairs of Jasper's house of the future, playing Frisbee across the wide concrete spaces. They got Madigan/Vivian to float outside like a kite, and stood there in the rain with her glowing green above them.

Later, when everything was quiet, and Mrs. Dash lit a fire in the fireplace with a small, handheld atom-smasher, they told stories of their adventures and talked about the future.

Katie was saying, "We should really go on a trip where we don't fight evil. Like I was saying back in Todburg. In a few years, we'll be able to drive ourselves. We could go to Mexico or something. Won't that be amazing? And we can listen to any music we want to in the car."

"We can already drive in a car," said Jasper. "We have our parents and my robot chauffeur."

"But it's *different*," said Katie. "It will be incredibly *cool*."

Lily, watching Mr. Gefelty and the Mulligans compare golf swings, said gradually, "Yeah . . . That will be cool. But I'm having fun right now. I don't . . . You know, I don't want to think about the future." She felt shy saying it, like a dork, because she should be wanting something better, some great, spectacular thing unknown and unimaginable, some image of wealth and maturity and snazz, but she couldn't really think of anything better than Katie and Jasper and Drgnan eating irradiated popcorn while the rain beat on the windows. Drgnan had a fully popped kernel in each nostril.

Lily thought about how she spent all her time preparing for something. She was always studying for a test so she could do well in school, and she was going to school so she could go to college, and she'd be going to college so she could get a job, and she would get a job so she could . . . She didn't even know yet. She hadn't thought that far ahead. But looking around the room at her mother, so happy to be back among the living,* and the other parents, Lily knew that *this* was why they had decided to have families. Parties like this. This was what they had pictured. Not just their kids all grown up, a finished product later on, but their children having a barbecue, and having friends, and being together at that moment. *Even,* she added to herself, looking tenderly at Jasper, *if one of our parents is just a highly concentrated beam of data projected from the region of the Horsehead Nebula.*

What mattered was not what they would become, but that they were together now.

So they sat and played stupid games, and outside the rain let up, because it was no longer a

---

*Fine, all right, so the title of this book is a little inaccurate. She was never exactly a "zombie" mommy. But then again, the title *Possessed-by-an-Off-Off-Broadway-Ghost-Actress Mommy* doesn't almost rhyme.

horror novel. Then the guests left. Lily sat in her car, with her mother beside her in the backseat, and they hugged each other tight. She thanked her mother for her necklace, and her mother cried. Jasper stood in the garage, scraping the grill as the guests drove away. He watched them as they went around the bend.

He closed the lid of the grill and grinned. It didn't matter when they would get old and when they would die.

They would think about the future when it came.

He did not go in until the green glow from Madigan, who was floating, tethered to the Mulligans' car, had become a mere speck in the distance and eventually was swallowed up in the night.